STORIES IN AN AGE OF FANTASY

KU-467-120

FORTRESS OF
GHOSTS

TOM HUDDLESTON

WARHAMMER ADVENTURES

First published in Great Britain in 2021 by
Warhammer Publishing,
Willow Road,
Nottingham, NG7 2WS, UK.

10 9 8 7 6 5 4 3 2 1

Produced by Games Workshop in Nottingham.
Cover illustration by Cole Marchetti.
Internal illustrations by Dan Boultwood & Cole Marchetti.

A CIP record for this book is available from the British Library.

ISBN 13: 978 1 78999 037 9

See Warhammer Adventures on the internet at

warhammeradventures.com

Find out more about Games Workshop and the worlds of
Warhammer 40,000 and Warhammer Age of Sigmar at

games-workshop.com

Printed and bound by CPI Group (UK) Ltd, Croydon, CR0 4YY

Contents

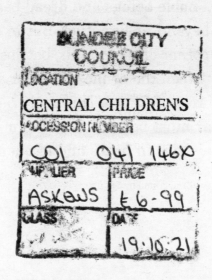

The Mortal Realms

Each of the Mortal Realms is a
world unto itself, steeped in powerful
magic. Seemingly infinite in size,
there are endless possibilities for
discovery and adventure: floating
cities and enchanted woodlands,
noble beings and dread beasts
beyond imagination. But in every
corner of the realms, battles rage
between the armies of Order and the
forces of Chaos. This centuries-long
war must be won if the realms are to
live in peace and freedom.

Seven days ago...

The air in Vertigan's study was dry and stifling and filled with a thousand ancient odours – foreign herbs and mystical powders, musty leather and dusty pages, tallow and coal and pipe smoke. Kaspar stepped in silently behind his companions, seeing books stacked to the ceiling, maps and parchments littering the ink-stained desk, racks and cases of weaponry and armour, some aged and rusting, some polished to a fine gleam.

The lantern flickered overhead and the horned manticore skull grimaced down as though it knew they weren't supposed to be there. They had no choice, though. Vertigan had been snatched by the Skaven, and they had to find a way to get him back.

'Who is this master of yours?' Kiri asked, looking around in amazement.

'He's a healer,' Elio told her.

'And a teacher,' Alish said softly.

'And I think he was a soldier once,' Thanis added.

Kaspar almost laughed, but bit it back. 'He's a witch hunter,' he said. 'None of you knew? I thought it was obvious.'

They turned to him, eyes wide. 'But witch hunters are creepy,' Alish protested. 'All dark and brooding and tough.'

'What, like Vertigan?' Kaspar pointed out. 'He's a member of the Order of Azyr, it's this secret group dedicated to Sigmar and the cause of peace. There were more of them in Lifestone once, scholars and soldiers and warrior-priests. They guarded the

Arbour so the healers could do their work.'

'So where did they all go?' Elio asked. 'And what made Vertigan stay?'

Kaspar shrugged. 'I don't know. It's not like Lifestone is teeming with... with...'

He broke off, his throat closing. Kiri looked at him, frowning. He shook his head.

'With witches to hunt. Sorry. Dry mouth.'

He turned away, hiding a sudden sense of confusion. The feeling in his throat hadn't been dryness exactly, it was as though for a brief moment cold fingers had tightened, trying to choke off his words. His hand scrabbled restlessly in his pocket and he drew it out. To his surprise he saw that he was clutching something, a small object made of black stone.

The pyramid. He'd almost forgotten.

He didn't know what it was, or where exactly it came from – Kiri had been given it by a strange woman in Lifestone, and told to pass it on to Kaspar. The woman had claimed to be his mother, but that was impossible – Kaspar's mother was long gone, along with the rest of his family. He'd been there when the fire took their home, he was the only one who'd managed to escape. So who was this strange woman, and what did she want with him?

He inspected the pyramid, turning it over in his palm. It wasn't entirely black, he noticed – there was a faint shimmering on the surface, lines and swirls of silver filigree that seemed to grow clearer as he stared at them. They made a shape, and as he looked closer he realised it was a rune – the mark of Shyish, Realm of Death. The same mark he bore on his wrist.

'Kaspar.'

The voice was clear and sudden, right next to his ear. He jumped, turning, but there was no one there. The others were inspecting something on Vertigan's desk, a large musty book.

'They can't hear me,' the voice said. It was a woman, calm and faintly amused. *'Only you can hear me. And only I can help you get your master back. Go somewhere quiet, where we won't be disturbed, and I'll tell you how.'*

Silently Kaspar backed towards the door. He glanced briefly at his friends – should he tell them what was happening? No, they had enough to worry about without thinking he was losing his mind. Until he knew what this was, he'd keep it to himself.

He stepped silently into the shadowed Atheneum. The huge domed hall was empty as he hurried across, fighting the urge to run. How could he run from something inside his head?

'You needn't be afraid,' the voice said. *'I won't hurt you, as long as you do as I say.'*

Kaspar descended the steps into the Arbour's basement, ducking into the passage that led to his room. He unhooked the tripwire that activated his soot-trap then he crossed the outer chamber, skirting the two covered pits in the floor and disarming the swinging sandbag that swept across the inner doorway. He lit a lantern with shaking hands then he placed the pyramid on his open palm, staring nervously down at it. The rune on its surface was clear now, glowing with a spectral light.

For a moment, all was silent. Had he been imagining things?

'The connection between us is strong,' the voice said loudly, and Kaspar jumped. *'Can you feel it?'*

'Wh-who are you?' he demanded. 'What do you want from me?'

The voice chuckled softly. *'I'm like you, Kaspar. I'm one of the chosen. In fact we share the same mark. The rune of Shyish.'*

'You took Vertigan,' Kaspar said, sure it was true. 'Where is he?'

'Your master is safe,' the voice said. *'And if you do exactly as I tell you,*

you'll see him again.'

'And what if I don't?' Kaspar hissed defiantly. 'What if I throw this stone away, run back upstairs and tell my friends that some witch tried to–'

A wave of burning cold ripped through his skull and Kaspar gasped with the force of it. He dropped to his knees on the stone floor as a blade of ice sliced behind his eyes. He heard his teeth chatter as all around him the walls of the room turned to smoke, coiling and swirling and breaking apart.

Through the fog he saw a dark landscape of black stone and low, dense mist. There were shadowy outlines in the gloom – carts and war machines, but all ruined, all burned. There were walls down there too, zigzag outlines against the dark rock, a great labyrinth shrouded in clouds of clinging vapour.

The view shifted and he was drifting towards some huge structure, a glass tower that rose from the black earth. Inside he could hear the noise of battle, screams and cries of fear and aggression. He rose up, up, and now he could see people in the gloom, a band of them, huddled together as a dark wave of fearsome phantoms bore down on them. They fought hard, but somehow Kaspar knew it was no good – the forces that assailed them were too strong, too numerous, too intent on destruction.

Then one of the group shouted, and even though he couldn't hear the words he recognised the voice. It was Thanis, her voice cracking with terror. Through the fog he saw her red hair gleaming, her cheeks flushed with effort. At her side were Alish and Kiri, and huddled behind them was Elio. And they were all in mortal danger, as the fell shapes tightened the cordon, moving inexorably inward.

Then suddenly he seemed to rise again, the scope of his vision widening, and he saw that beyond his tiny group of besieged friends, beyond the ring of their attackers, beyond the tower and the misted maze, something else moved. Something vast and dark and restless. Something with ten thousand feet and a single hideous purpose.

'The army of the dead,' the voice said, and Kaspar felt his breath stop.

'They're coming here,' he realised. 'They're coming to Lifestone. But why?'

'To take back what is mine,' the voice told him. *'To claim this land in my name. All that you have seen here will come to pass, if you do not do as I command.'*

Kaspar shuddered, remembering the fear on Thanis's face. 'But who are you?' he demanded. 'Please, tell me!'

'I am Ashnakh!'

The vision before him suddenly broke, the walls of his room slamming back into place as though some force had driven them together. But now he was no longer alone – a woman stood on the stone tiles, hooded and cloaked and all in black.

She drew back her hood and he
gasped at her beauty. Her face was
like something from a tale, her lips the
deepest crimson, her hair the darkest
ebony. Her smile was like moonrise over
a graveyard.

'I am Ashnakh,' she repeated. 'The
feared and the loved. Scourge of the
Ghastlands. Victor at the Battle of the
Seven Weeping Rivers. Queen of the
Castle of Mirrors, and faithful servant
of Nagash, the Lord of Death.'

'Wh... why are you here?' Kaspar

asked, fighting the urge to cower before her.

'I told you, we have a connection,' Ashnakh said, exposing her wrist. There on the pale skin was the same mark he bore, an angled line with a wave curling from it. 'A bond between us. I hoped it would make you more... receptive to my offer.'

Kaspar frowned. 'What offer? When will you take me to Vertigan?'

'Soon, child. You're almost all here, aren't you? Lifestone's chosen. There's just one left to find, then the circle will be complete.'

'The circle?' Kaspar asked. 'Why do we have these marks? Vertigan never told us.'

'They're for a ritual,' the sorceress said. 'A grand spell of making and unmaking, and the time has almost come.'

Kaspar shook his head. His thoughts were growing clouded, his will weakening. 'What do you want from me?' he pleaded.

'Very little,' Ashnakh said. 'Just your eyes and your ears. The marks will lead you to the sixth child. All you need to do is stay alert, and whatever your friends decide to do, go along. I'll see every move you make, thanks to our special link.'

'You want me to spy on my friends?' Kaspar asked. 'No. I won't do it.'

Ashnakh's smile broke, her eyes flashing, her cloak billowing. Kaspar felt lightning in the air and heard a cold, distant howling.

'You will,' she said. 'If you ever want to see Vertigan again, you will. If you want to keep your friends alive and avoid the fate you witnessed in my vision, you will. I could end their lives any time I wanted, I could stop their hearts like that.'

She snapped her fingers and he saw purple sparks leaping, reflected in her black eyes. In her shadow he felt small, helpless, utterly overwhelmed.

'I'll see everything you do,' she said.

'I'll hear everything you say.'

A thought flashed into Kaspar's mind – *can you feel what I feel, too? Do you know what I'm thinking?* But Ashnakh did not react.

'I will be with you every step,' she said, her anger abating. 'We're connected, Kaspar. We're bonded, now and forever.'

He looked up at her and felt a strange, unearthly calm come over him. Here was a power greater than anything he'd witnessed before, greater even than Vertigan's. He could try to resist it, he could try to fight, but deep down he knew it would be hopeless. She was a great sorceress and he was merely a child. A thief. A sneak.

He had no doubt that Ashnakh would do as she threatened – she would crush him, and his friends too if he defied her. Thanis would suffer the fate he'd witnessed, all of them would be lost. He had only one choice.

Slowly, he got down onto one knee.

'Mistress Ashnakh,' he said. 'I am yours to command.'

CHAPTER ONE

The Battlerock

As the sun sank, the seas of Shyish turned red as blood.

Kaspar stood on the quarterdeck of the huge black ship, staring out across the rolling waves. Dark shapes moved beneath the water, tentacles coiled to the surface and sank from sight, nested eyes glinting in the depths. Something large brushed against the side of the ship; he felt the deck tremble with the force of it.

On the outer rigging one of the deadwalker sailors lost his footing, bony fingers snatching at the ropes as he fell. He landed on his back in the

water, empty eye sockets staring up.
Then a dark form rose, black teeth
bared in a rotted grey maw, a tattered
fin hanging limp in the red light. The
dead shark took the sailor in its gaping
jaws, and Kaspar heard the crack of
bones.

He turned away, his stomach roiling.
They'd reached the Realm of Death
three days earlier, passing through
a Realmgate shaped like a giant
water-tornado, which had swirled the
ship and its crew up into the glittering
skies of Chamon and dropped them
with a splash into the Sea of Fading
Hope, one of the vast oceans of Shyish.

Kaspar had felt queasy ever since, and
not just from seasickness. The air felt
heavy somehow, clammy and oppressive.
The presence of all these walking
corpses disgusted him; their rotting
frames and bony hands, their grinning,
empty skulls. Even the pyramid around
his neck seemed to have grown heavier,
its dragging weight reminding him of

all the choices he'd made to get here.

But at least he could breathe free. Down on the main deck a large wooden crate stood lashed with rope. There were small holes in the top but no windows, no bars. His companions had been locked inside since Ashnakh had captured them, and he could only imagine how they'd been suffering. They'd survive, they were strong, but it must be miserable in there.

'You don't have to worry about them any more,' Ashnakh said, and Kaspar started. She'd have made a good thief, he thought; she moved even more softly than he did. Perhaps it had something to do with being undead. 'They made their choice. They chose to defy me and now they're paying the price. We all are.' She sighed bitterly.

'I tried to stop Scratch from jumping,' Kaspar said. 'I failed you, mistress.'

'That foolish, frightened child,' the sorceress snarled. 'How could he have been so reckless? And now all my work is ruined, all my plans come to nothing. All we can do is wait until another is called. Still, my lord is nothing if not patient.'

Kaspar shuddered. Ashnakh was doing all of this for her master, Nagash, the Lord of Death. It was for him that she'd tracked down the six marked children, luring them with the promise of finding their own mentor, Vertigan. But she'd pushed too hard and one of them had snapped: the feral boy known as Scratch had leapt over the railing of the ship, shocking them all. Now Ashnakh was determined to keep the rest of them imprisoned until another marked child was called, even if it took years.

The sun dipped below the horizon and in the stillness Kaspar heard the splash and slither of a million slimy things. A flock of ragged birds passed over, oily feathers clinging to their skeletal pinions, their hoarse moans echoing over the water. But they soared too low and a huge rotting tongue uncoiled

from the ocean, lashing around one of
the birds and dragging it, screeching,
from the sky.

Then he saw a flash of light and
raised his head. Ahead of them a vast
shape rose from the water – a stony
island, large and dark, hunched like a
sleeping troggoth over the black sea.
Pale mists gathered on its shores and
in the depths he saw that light again,
a golden flare glancing through the fog.

'Is it a lighthouse?' he asked. He'd
read about them in a story once.

Ashnakh shook her head. 'That is your
new home. My Castle of Mirrors.'

She made a gesture and the fog
banks parted, rolling back over the
rugged rocks. On the clifftops a great
spire was revealed, a tower so tall that
its upper levels were still in sunlight,
sending shafts of red light across
the churning sea. But why were the
light-beams moving? Kaspar shielded
his eyes, took a closer look, and finally
understood.

The Castle of Mirrors was aptly
named – every part of it was
constructed from vast sheets of glass,
each one bigger than the last. But
somehow they were floating free,
unconnected to one another, the entire
structure slowly revolving. As they
moved the mirrors caught the sun's last
radiance, casting it out into the evening
air in a glancing dance of ghostly light.

He gripped the railing, remembering
the vision Ashnakh had shown him,

that night at the Arbour. The castle was terrifying but it was beautiful too, a sight more majestic than any he'd seen. He could barely imagine stepping inside it, but a part of him couldn't wait to.

He heard the crash of waves and the creak of timbers, and as they drew closer to the island he saw the wrecks of sunken ships on either side, broken prows jutting from the water. A figurehead rose, sculpted like a warrior woman, but so rotten now that her eyes were black holes, her mouth a twisted grimace.

The corpse sailors worked the ropes, lowering the sails with a snap and a creak. One of them got his foot caught, and tried desperately to pull himself free as he was dragged towards a spinning winch. But it was too late: the rope snapped as the deadwalker flew to pieces, his skull skittering across the deck.

Then there was a thump, and the

ship stopped dead. Peering over the railing Kaspar saw a stone pier clinging to the cliff face. Ropes dropped from the side of the ship, lashed to the jetty by gangs of skeletal dock workers. They had arrived.

On the deck he saw deadwalkers swarming all over the wooden crate, tying ropes and tightening chains. It rose into the air, lifted by a large crane-arm that swung out over the dock. Kaspar heard a muffled cry and turned away.

'Come,' Ashnakh said, taking his arm. They descended the gangplank, Kaspar's stomach turning as he touched solid ground. Above him he saw the crate swinging off the dock, being lowered onto a wooden cart.

Ashnakh raised her hands, weaving them in the air and whispering soft words. Against the cliff wall Kaspar saw a pile of white fragments. He'd thought they were pale pieces of stone, but now they began to rise, floating and spinning. They were bones, he realised, legs and ribs and skulls, all coming together to form a pair of large, four-legged shapes, their heads bowed as they faced Ashnakh.

She clicked her tongue and the skeletal horses stepped forward, their hooves clopping on the stone jetty. One approached Kaspar, lowering its fleshless snout. A saddle was placed on its back and Ashnakh gestured, mounting her own steed. 'It won't bite,' she said. 'Unless I want it to.'

Kaspar looked into the horse's empty eye socket and tried to understand. Did the creature know what it was, or *if* it was? Was there a mind in there, or a soul? Might this be his fate some day, to be a collection of bones enslaved to Ashnakh, unable to think for himself?

Shivering, he took hold of the bridle, hoisting himself up. Ashnakh's horse advanced and Kaspar followed, looking down through the creature's undulating ribcage to the stones beneath. A whip cracked and the cart drew in behind them, pulled by a line of straining deadwalkers.

A path wound across the cliff, just wide enough for the cart and its unsteady burden. Light shimmered below and Kaspar realised that the track was made from fragments of shattered glass, reflecting the light of the rising moon. Then they reached the top, and he looked out over the scorched landscape of the island.

'Its name is the Battlerock,' Ashnakh said. 'And it is my dominion.'

In the far distance the ground rose, a bare ridge crossing the centre of the island. To Kaspar's left the Castle of Mirrors stood tall on the cliff edge, dark panes circling. All around it lay a dense layer of mist, hugging the foot of the tower and coiling outwards in every direction. The path led towards it, vanishing into the gloom.

'Stay close, and do not stray,' Ashnakh told Kaspar as they approached the fog bank. Tendrils of vapour coiled around the horses' hooves. 'This is no ordinary mist. We are entering the Shatterglass Labyrinth, there are spells here to confuse the mind and baffle the senses. If you lose yourself, even I might not be able to find you again.'

Shapes rose on either side, dark walls closing them in. But these were not stone barricades, Kaspar saw – they were formed from shards of broken glass, huge fractured panes reflecting the moon, and the mist, and each other. The track split and split again, countless small ways branching from the wider path. But Ashnakh held her course, her undead steed moving slowly, purposefully through the fog.

Kaspar shivered, imagining what it would be like to lose himself in that pale, drifting emptiness. Then he heard a sound and turned sharply. It was a shout, or many shouts, muffled by the mist. It came again and he heard the clash of swords, and the fearful whinnying of horses. In the mirrors he saw movement – the spectral forms of warriors, almost lost in the shadows.

'The Battlerock is aptly named,' Ashnakh told him. 'There was a mighty conflict here once, and its echoes still remain. Two vast armies came together, fighting so long and so hard that when they were done nothing was left alive, not an insect, not a shrub, not a blade of grass. And so it remains, centuries later. This is a dead place.'

'But why here?' Kaspar asked. 'Why fight over this lump of rock?'

'Because of that,' Ashnakh said, pointing between the mirrored walls,

above the shifting fog, towards the centre of the island. At first Kaspar could see nothing, just the stony ridge lifting towards the clouds. But then he saw a purple shimmer in the air above it, rising from the dark stones.

'A Realmgate,' he said. 'The one that links to Rawdeep Mere!'

Ashnakh smiled. 'Clever boy. This island is of huge strategic importance, that is why my lord Nagash entrusted it to me. And he gave me a purpose, too. A prize to win, a city to claim. My home.'

'Lifestone,' Kaspar said. 'This is where your army marched from.'

'It is,' Ashnakh nodded. 'And very

soon, you will understand why.'

She tugged on the reins and the skeletal steed halted, the cart grinding to a stop behind them. One of the undead hauliers took out a crowbar, plunging it into a crack in the side of the crate. He heaved and the side wall worked loose, dropping with a crash. For a long moment there was silence. Kaspar felt his heart pound.

Then Thanis and Kiri jumped down together, arms linked as they hit the ground. They looked at the mist surrounding them, the mirrored walls rising, the deadwalkers standing in dumb silence. Then they saw Ashnakh and Kaspar, and Thanis's eyes flashed with loathing.

'So this is Shyish,' Alish said, clambering down behind them.

Elio followed, shivering. 'It's pretty much what I expected. Cold, dreary.'

'And full of evil things,' Thanis added, her eyes still on Kaspar.

Ashnakh snorted. 'Look around you,

children. The Battlerock is a place of wonders. Witness, my Castle of Mirrors.'

They peered up at the great tower, shimmering in the moonlight. Alish's mouth fell open but she shut it again quickly.

'Personally,' she said, 'I preferred the Kharadron sky-city.'

'Or the Elmheart Glade,' Elio agreed. 'That was much more impressive.'

'Silence!' Ashnakh snapped. 'You are in the heart of the Shatterglass Labyrinth, a place from which there is no escape. Here you will wait until I have need of you again.'

Kiri looked around, then back up at Ashnakh. 'So you want us to just wander about? That doesn't sound so bad.'

Ashnakh smiled, waving a hand. 'Yes, be my guest. Roam. Explore. Lose yourselves in the labyrinth. There is no way out, though I know that won't stop you from searching. Oh, but you should know one thing. You're not alone.'

She coiled her fingers and the mist shifted around them, swirling upwards from the ground, forming dark and nebulous shapes. Kaspar felt a chill in his bones, a heaviness in his heart. He heard a wail and the rattle of chains.

'My nighthaunts,' Ashnakh whispered. 'Beautiful, aren't they?'

Spectral shapes emerged from the mist like something from the deepest nightmare. They were hooded figures, with long, bony arms and skull-like faces. Each was wrapped in clanking chains, and some also carried weapons – notched swords, rusted daggers and long-bladed scythes.

Thanis gritted her teeth. 'You won't let them kill us,' she said. 'You need us alive to perform this ritual of yours.'

Ashnakh's smile broadened. 'No, they won't kill you,' she admitted as the spectres closed in. 'But of course, murder is not a chainghast's specialty.'

'Wh... what is?' Alish asked as the rattling grew louder.

Ashnakh chuckled, and slowly her head turned. Kaspar looked up in surprise as her eyes fixed directly on his.

'Fear,' she said. 'Fear is how I will control you.'

He felt a chill on his back, a shiver rising. Tearing his eyes from Ashnakh he looked over his shoulder and cried out in shock.

The nighthaunt had approached so silently that he hadn't noticed it; now it was almost upon him, its rictus mouth open in silent laughter, its bone-fingered hands weaving as it came. The terror that gripped Kaspar was more intense than anything he'd ever felt: he could barely move, barely speak, waves of fear coursing like cold mercury through his veins.

'Mistress, no,' he managed. 'Haven't I done everything you asked of me? Haven't I been faithful to you?'

Ashnakh snorted softly. 'Of course you have, dear Kaspar. But one can never be too careful.'

The apparition reached out, and the last thing Kaspar heard before the darkness overcame him was his own voice, desperately shrieking.

CHAPTER TWO

Darkwing

Kaspar screamed in silence, lost in a
whirlwind of fear. He writhed helplessly,
his mind struggling for clarity as winds
of terror buffeted him. He could see
that ghastly thing wherever he looked,
its grasping fingers, its hooded cowl, its
empty, eyeless sockets. It was as though
it was inside him, part of him, his own
ghostly reflection.

His eyes seemed to open, but at first
all he could see was darkness. Then
he saw that there were shapes in the
black, circling him, flickering. They
were mirrors, each as tall as himself,
revolving in the emptiness through

which he drifted. He stared into them, searching for his own image, for anything to tell him who he was.

A face stared back. It was a perfect face, pale as milk, with red lips and hair of obsidian, smiling from the whirling mirrors. Ashnakh's face, with his own buried deep inside. Somewhere music played, a chiming melody that he knew somehow, a song dragged up from the deepest recesses of his memory. Or was it her memory?

He reached up, touching his cheeks, his nose, his lips. His skin felt hard, like glass. He tried to open his mouth but he was too brittle; if he pushed too hard he'd break. He was transparent, empty, his spirit fluttering inside like a moth trapped in a bottle.

'Break the glass.'

The voice was calm, close by. It was a man, someone he knew. He looked into the mirrors again, searching for something, anything that might help him.

Vertigan's face stared back, and his

eyes shone with warmth and love.
'Break the glass, Kaspar,' he said.
'You're the only one who can.'

Kaspar felt the breath inside him,
rising through his glass throat, between
his glass teeth. He forced his mouth
open and felt his cheeks shatter, heard
the crack and splinter as he began to
break apart. He forced the sound up,
out, waiting to hear himself scream into
the void.

But instead, the only sound that
emerged was the hoarse cry of a bird.

He felt a sharp pain in his head and
opened his eyes.

The black eye was barely a palm's
breadth from his own, and for a
moment Kaspar was sure he was still
dreaming. Then the raven blinked and
he reacted, pushing it away, struggling
to sit up. The bird cawed angrily,
taking to the air and landing a short
distance away, watching him.

Kaspar looked around. He was in a

bed piled with soft linens, in the centre
of a grand, circular room patterned
with shafts of moving light. The walls
were mirrored, and as he looked he
could see himself reflected countless
times, receding into infinity. But at
least his face was his own.

He reached up to touch his forehead,
feeling a sore spot right in the centre
where the bird had pecked him. 'She
sent you to wake me, did she?'

The bird nodded its head, clinging to
the perch.

Unsteadily, Kaspar got to his feet. He could see himself reflected in the floor, his pale legs and his underthings and the filthy soles of his feet. The outer wall revolved slowly and he crossed to it. The gaps between the panes let in beams of pale sunlight. Peering through he could see the restless ocean and the slopes of Battlerock Island. Directly below was the labyrinth, a blanket of mist with dark shapes poking through. His friends were down there, he knew. Lost and afraid. Well, there was nothing he could do for them now.

The raven squawked, gesturing with its beak, and he saw that it was perched on a metal clothes rack, its claws grasping the cloth of his robe. It twisted its head, pecking at something, lifting it. It was the pyramid pendant, dangling from a leather cord. Kaspar reached out and took it, slipping the cord around his neck.

You're awake. Ashnakh's voice tore through his skull like a shout. The

intensity of their bond had increased –
here in her own domain, everything
about Ashnakh seemed magnified. *'And
you met Darkwing.'*

'It pecked me,' Kaspar complained, and
Ashnakh laughed.

*'He was like you, once. Weren't you,
my pet? He was human. But he tried to
trick me, and look what happened.'*

The raven cawed simperingly, then
it spread its black wings to their full
extent, leaning forward as though
bowing. Kaspar saw a silver outline on
the dark feathers – the same rune of
Shyish that he and Ashnakh bore.

*'Now he's my faithful servant, just
as you are,'* the sorceress said. *'So you
must try to get along. Dress yourself
and meet me at the base of the spiral
stairs. There is much I need to show
you.'*

Kaspar felt the connection sever, as
though an invisible candle had been
snuffed out inside his head. The raven
stood smirking, pecking at its feathers.

Kaspar swiped at it.

'Filthy creature,' he said. 'Flap off and leave me alone.'

The bird flew towards an arched doorway, perching on a pane of glass and cawing insistently. Kaspar remembered the nighthaunt's bony fingers against his skin and shuddered.

'Don't worry,' he told the raven. 'I'll do as I'm told.'

Darkwing swooped away into the passage, its squawk fading. Kaspar tugged on his robe and shoes, feeling exhausted despite his long sleep. There was a bowl of dark fruit on the table but he didn't feel like eating. Beside it was a tumbler of cool water; it tasted musty and unpleasant, as though drawn from a graveyard well. He turned to follow the raven, and that was when he heard the sound.

It was just a low hiss at first, a susurrating whisper like something breathing. For the briefest moment he thought he saw a shape in the mirrors, a dark form flitting out of sight.

'Is... is someone there?' he asked. 'Show yourself.'

Silence fell. The only movement was the sunlight slanting between the walls. Then a shadow darted behind him, reflected in the mirror he was facing, and he whirled round.

'What are you? Another spy for the mistress? Or just dirt on the glass?'

The hiss came again, and this time there were words in it. 'Neeeither,' it whispered. 'We must ssspeak with you, Kasssspar.'

The shadow in the glass darkened, forming a huddled shape. It looked like a human figure, but one glimpsed through a melting sheet of ice – the features were indistinct, the outline always changing. And it wasn't alone, Kaspar saw, there were others behind it, weaving and warping like reflections in water.

'You're *children*,' he realised out loud.

'We were,' the first figure said, his voice gaining clarity. 'Long ago.'

'How did you get here?' Kaspar asked. 'How did you end up in this mirror?'

'It is no ordinary mirror.' This was a girl's voice, and he matched it to a blue blur with flickering eyes. 'This substance is called shadeglass. It traps spirits.'

'Many of Ashnakh's victims are here,' another boy said, drifting so close to the glass that Kaspar could make out sunken yellow eyes in a gaunt, pale face.

'But we were the first.' A second girl

spoke; she had copper-coloured skin and night-black hair. A fifth figure lurked silently behind her skirts, clasping a tatty shape that might've been a rag doll. Kaspar couldn't tell if it was a boy or a girl.

'How long have you been here?' he asked.

'We don't know,' the first boy admitted. 'Time has no meaning in the mirror. Long enough to forget our names, our lives, our pasts...'

Kaspar edged towards the door. 'Look, I've been summoned and I really don't want to make Ashnakh mad on my first day.' He stepped into the passage but the spectral children kept pace, darting through the mirrors that lined the hallway, moving from one floating pane to the next.

'You must listen,' the first boy said. 'We need your help.'

Kaspar looked at him. 'I'm loyal to Ashnakh. Why would I help you?'

'We can assist you in return. We can

help you find your way. There are many dangers in the Castle of Mirrors.'

Kaspar eyed him closely but the boy's features were too indistinct to accurately gauge his expression. 'How do I know you aren't playing games? That this isn't another loyalty test of Ashnakh's?'

The blue girl hissed. 'If she knew we'd shown ourselves to you... there are things she could do. Pain she could inflict. We would not have spoken unless we were truly desperate.'

'Even now you could hurt us,' the pale boy added. 'If you told her...'

'What makes you think I won't?' Kaspar demanded.

The dark girl smiled faintly. 'Because we don't think you're as bad as you seem.'

Kaspar gritted his teeth, wrestling with his doubts. Then he shook his head. 'You're wrong,' he said. 'There's nothing I can do for you. Now leave me alone.'

He lowered his head and marched along the hallway, heading for what he hoped was the centre of the castle. Soon the corridor opened out, passing beneath a large, mirrored archway. He stepped through, and his throat tightened in horror.

The landing on which he stood was halfway up a vast spiral staircase that wound right around the inside wall of the castle. Above and below he could see other doorways, other passages opening and closing as the mirrors moved. But ahead of him, filling the long open shaft in the centre of the tower like the core in a coal-apple, was a column of bones.

It rose before him, huge and white and gleaming, thousands upon thousands of interlocking skulls, legs, arms, fingers. Some were massive, the horned carapaces and armoured breastbones of gargants and griffons, manticores and sky-wyrms. But many more were recognisably human, the

bones arranged in hideous patterns,
shoulder blades spread like wings
surrounding spirals of separated jaws,
or rows of straight femurs arranged to
form blocks and squares and geometric
shapes. It was like an artwork created
by a crazed, inhuman beast, the
product of an utterly twisted mind.

The steps on which he stood were
part of it too, jutting from the central
pillar like ribs from some monstrous
spinal column. And like a spine, the
tower also appeared to be hollow – he
could see light inside, hazy and moving,
slicing through empty eye sockets or
between cracks in the bones. He took a
step closer.

'Kaspar, don't.'

The voice came from behind him,
and turning he saw the ghost children
watching from the mirrored outer
wall. The stark difference between
the smooth brilliance of the mirrors
and the gruesome horror of the bone
tower struck him then – it was such

a hideous clash, and yet somehow it made sense. It was all cold, and hard, and dead.

'Do not look inside,' the tall boy said. 'What you'll see is more dreadful than you can imagine. You're in a lot of trouble, Kaspar. But we can help you.'

Kaspar glanced back at the bone pillar, wondering what it could possibly contain that was worse than all this. Then he shook his head.

'Just leave me alone,' he said.

Then he started down the spiral stairway, leaving them behind. It wasn't long before he saw Ashnakh standing below him, tapping one leather-booted foot impatiently. He picked up the pace, forcing a smile onto his face.

CHAPTER THREE

The Shatterglass
Labyrinth

The nighthaunt screeched and circled
back towards them, a ragged cloak of
mist streaming out behind. Kiri gripped
Thanis's ankles, ducking as the cackling
phantom swept overhead. *They're toying
with us*, she thought. *And they're
enjoying it.*

'We have to stop.' Elio's voice was
hoarse behind her as the apparition
vanished into the labyrinth. She felt
her burden shift and turned to see him
dropping Thanis's arms and sinking
down onto the bare, damp earth. 'I

can't go on. She's too heavy.'

Alish stood over them, her face tight with fear. Thanis lay sprawled on the ground, her eyes open but sightless.

The nighthaunt had crept up on her just before dawn as she was keeping lookout, trying to buy time so the others could snatch a few moments' sleep. Kiri had heard a shriek and awoken to find Thanis curled up and whimpering. She'd slipped into unconsciousness soon after, and since then they'd been forced to carry her. For Kiri it wasn't so bad, she could hoist Thanis's ankles up under her arms and keep moving. But Elio didn't have her strength, however hard he tried.

'They're coming back,' Alish said, glancing fearfully back along the pathway formed by the broken mirrors. Shattered panes rose on either side of them, ghost-lights flickering in their blank depths.

'Of course they are,' Elio said, his

voice cracking. 'And they'll keep coming, and coming, forever and ever and–'

'Don't.' Alish put a hand on his arm. 'Not forever. Just until the next mark is called.'

'Which could be years,' Elio pointed out. 'Do you really think we could survive for years in this place? We'll lose our minds.'

'We're going to escape,' Kiri said firmly. 'There has to be a way. There's always a way.'

'You don't know that,' Elio said. 'How could you know that?'

'I broke out of a Darkoath slave camp,' Kiri told him. 'And we all got out of Kreech's warren.'

'But Ashnakh's not some barbarian, and she's certainly not a stupid Skaven,' Elio argued. 'She's a sorceress. A necromancer. She's got *power*.'

Kiri grinned ruefully. 'So have I. Come on, I'll carry Thanis.'

She hefted the girl over her shoulder like a sack of grain and they staggered on, trying to ignore the nighthaunts moaning in the fog. Elio was right, it wasn't going to be easy to find a way out of Ashnakh's labyrinth. The mirrored walls weren't the only thing keeping them here, Kiri was convinced. The whole place was filled with dark magic.

All night they'd heard screams and cries, the din of some invisible battle. They'd seen forms in the mirrors – figures and faces, creatures and carts and even piles of food, so real that Kiri had stepped forward, hand outstretched, only to bruise her knuckles on the hard surface.

Their only point of reference, the only solid object in this formless place, was the Castle of Mirrors itself. It rose from the centre of the fog bank, its surface rippling as the sun lifted. But they couldn't seem to get any closer to it; every time they moved it seemed to as well. They were every bit as lost as Elio said they were.

But Kiri refused to give up.
Ashnakh was powerful, but she wasn't
omnipotent. She had a weakness,
everyone did, and Kiri was determined
to find it.

The nighthaunt rose suddenly
in front of her and she retreated,
struggling to balance Thanis's weight
on her shoulders, one hand fumbling
instinctively for her catapult. But it
was gone, taken by Ashnakh's corpse
slaves. They were defenceless.

She lurched out of the way as the
phantom swept by, its hissing laugh
chilling her to the bone. It was
more full-bodied than most of the
chainghasts, its floating legs lashed at
the ankles. Its arms were tied behind
its back but it snapped at Elio with
bared teeth, making him jerk back in
terror.

Then Alish made a surprised sound
and Kiri looked her way. The girl was
fumbling in her pockets, muttering
excitedly.

'She didn't take them. I really don't think she took them.'

She yanked her hand free, whipping it outwards just as the nighthaunt was about to lay its hands on Elio. There was a bang and a flare of light and the spectre drew back, hissing. It didn't go far, but Alish threw another one of her Bolts of Azyr and the nighthaunt retreated again.

Kiri shifted her burden as they ran, the angry nighthaunt turning in pursuit.

'It seems to be... wary of fire,' Elio managed between breaths. 'Perhaps we should... try to set light to... something.'

'Like what?' Kiri managed. 'Everything's dead.'

'How about that?' Alish pointed.

A black shape rose from the mist, and for a moment Kiri thought it was some new kind of apparition. But then she saw that it was perfectly still – a weathered tree, perched on a rocky rise. Dead like everything else, but still standing.

She angled towards it, bent almost double. 'It's worth a try.'

The knoll below the tree was bare and exposed, roots winding into the ground. They struggled up the slope, but as they did so Kiri saw more movement up ahead and skidded to a stop, the weight on her shoulders almost dragging her off her feet. Two nighthaunts drifted down through the branches, their dark cloaks coiling soundlessly. One carried a lantern, a sickly green glow leaking from it, while the other swung a reaper's scythe, cutting the mist into spiralling tendrils.

Kiri glanced over her shoulder. The first spectre was still following, weaving through the mist. They were caught between them. She set Thanis carefully on the ground and the three of them bunched together on the rocky hillock.

'How many bolts have you got?' Kiri asked Alish.

The girl fumbled in her pocket,
pulling out a single twist of cloth. She
gulped. 'I'd better make it count.'

The nighthaunts began to circle,
drifting around them in a shrinking
pattern, like a tightening noose. Alish
clasped the bolt in her hand, kissing
her knuckles for luck. Then she drew
back and let fly.

One of the nighthaunts swung its
scythe, trying to knock the tiny object
off course. But it was too slow – the
Bolt of Azyr struck the base of the

tree, exploding with a bright flash. There was a deafening sound, a great roaring WHOOMPH, and Kiri was blinded by a wave of golden light.

She shielded her eyes, feeling the heat on her face. The entire tree was on fire, flames rushing up from the lower branches, consuming the smaller twigs at the top. The heat rose, driving the fog back, and for a second she could see beyond the labyrinth, across the stone plains of the island to a high black ridge. There was something in the air above it, a haze, a shimmering violet colour...

Then the nighthaunts shrieked and she turned back. The phantoms had drawn away, bony arms raised over their shining skulls. They fled into the fog, howls echoing through the mist.

'It worked,' Alish said breathlessly.

Elio squeezed her shoulder. 'Great shot. Couldn't have done better myself.'

'Now let's get out of here before those things return,' Kiri said, stooping.

'Wait,' Elio muttered. 'I think we're too late.'

Kiri followed his gaze. There was another dark shape in the fog, coalescing as it moved towards them. She felt her heart sink – could nothing hold those creatures off?

Then she heard a noise like boots striking the hard ground. The mist parted and a tall figure was revealed, hurtling towards them, waving its arms and letting out a string of unintelligible sounds. It was a man, Kiri saw, with tangled hair and a skinny, starved frame. He slowed his pace, staring frantically at the three children.

'What is this?' he demanded, gesturing at the tree. 'A sign? A beacon? Why have you come?'

Alish clutched Kiri's hand but Elio stepped forward. 'We came to find you,' he said in wonder. 'We came for you, Master Vertigan.'

Kiri gasped. He was right. They had found their master.

Vertigan faced them, his wide eyes glistening in the firelight. 'Begone, spirits,' he hissed. 'Why do you insist on tormenting me?'

'But master, it's us,' Alish said. 'We're not spirits.'

Vertigan shook his head. 'You're ghosts,' he spat. 'Just like the last ones. They begged for my help, but they were only figments of my imagination.'

'We're not figments,' Kiri insisted, holding out a hand. 'Here, touch. I'm real.'

Vertigan sniffed, his nostrils twitching.
His skin was pasty and his hair fell
in a lank tumble over his shoulders.
He reached out gingerly, touching Kiri's
hand then darting back.

'Doesn't prove anything. This place is
filled with spells.' He shook his head,
muttering under his breath. 'Not safe.
Not safe out here. Need to get to cover,
before they come back. Get to cover.'

'You know a place to hide?' Kiri
asked.

Vertigan laughed, a thin, hoarse
cackle. 'Hide, yes. Hide, and forget
about spectres, and ghosts, and all that
was before.'

Suddenly he sprang forward, bounding
into the fog.

CHAPTER FOUR

Bloodspeed

The mirrored track wound into the hills
and the dead horses followed. Ashnakh
led the way while Kaspar trotted
dutifully behind, trying not to notice
how splinters of bone kept flaking off
his mount every time he kicked his
spurs. The raven, Darkwing, perched
on its mistress's shoulder, glancing
back at Kaspar with a glint in its
black eye, like it knew something it
shouldn't know. It made him decidedly
uncomfortable.

They had picked their way through
the mists of the labyrinth, following
tracks and trails that only Ashnakh

knew. Kaspar had looked for signs of his companions, but had seen nothing except for a strange glimmer at one point – a distant glow, like something burning. Then it was gone. Now they were back on open ground, heading for the heart of the Battlerock. All around on the island's slopes were the remnants of what must have been a great host – pits and cart-tracks, abandoned workshops and stone-cold forges, tattered banners planted crooked in the earth. But these weren't ancient remains, they were fresh. An army had camped here, and very recently.

They came over a last rise and looked up towards the central ridge, and Kaspar felt waves of sickening power rolling down towards him. That purple gleam was in the air again, familiar from his time at Rawdeep Mere. Shielding his eyes, he could make out the source of it.

The warpstone crystal was so huge it had torn a hole between the realms, sunk into the stone of the island like the bright pupil in a great black eye. In its centre was an opening, a tunnel bored into the crystal itself, and it was towards this that their path led. He could see movement in and around this hollowed passage – deadwalker slaves erecting scaffolds and stanchions, while more emerged pushing carts and barrows heaped with mud. There was a deep gulping sound and water spilled from the tunnel, carrying with it toppled deadwalkers and a number of large, silvery fish, writhing and gasping on the rocky ground.

'The gate to Ghyran,' Kaspar said, and Ashnakh nodded.

'On one side death, on the other life. A perfect balance. At least until your friends came and ruined everything. Days of work it's taken to drain the lake and excavate the gate again. But we're almost there.'

'I'm sorry,' Kaspar muttered. 'I'd have stopped them if I could, but you said...'

'I said to go along with whatever they did,' Ashnakh agreed. 'I underestimated their determination to make my life difficult. But they're paying for it now, believe me. And it won't make any difference, my dark army will still have their prize.'

She gestured, and Kaspar took a sharp breath. He'd been so distracted by the light from the Realmgate that he hadn't even glanced at the shadowed slopes below. Now he looked, and marvelled at what he saw.

He'd assumed that the majority of Ashnakh's forces had passed through the gate before his friends closed it; the army besieging Lifestone was already huge. But it was nothing to the host now gathered on the hillside beneath the warpstone peak. The majority were skeletal warriors, their bones gleaming white, standing perfectly still as Kaspar and Ashnakh rode closer. They were dormant, he realised, waiting for their mistress's signal to move, to march, to fight. They each clutched a rusted short-sword, and some wore helmets or scraps of leather armour, dry and ancient and rotting. Several were missing limbs, hands and feet; even heads.

Up on the higher slopes he could see a dark purple marquee, its canvas sides stirring in the feeble breeze. A group of soulblight vampire generals stood before it, their armour gleaming in the watery sunlight, surveying the troops gathered below them. And all around the fringes a pale fog clung, crowded with dim shapes – nighthaunts, waiting in formless ranks for the mistress's command.

The track led between the rows of skeletal soldiers, and Kaspar heard the scrape of bone as, rank by rank, the undead soldiers turned to watch the sorceress passing.

'I don't understand,' he said carefully. 'I thought your plans were on hold, I thought that when Scratch–'

'Don't speak that creature's name,' Ashnakh snapped. 'Yes, his foolishness forced me to rethink my plans. The ritual cannot be completed until the next marked child is called, whenever that might be. I considered bringing my army home, gathering our strength until the time comes. But the thought of it *disgusted* me. That foul city, living on while I lingered here, day after day, just waiting. And who knows what could happen in the meantime – those despicable Sylvaneth could rise against me, your friends could make trouble in ways I cannot yet foresee.

'No, Lifestone must fall. Its time has come. I'll garrison it with my dead army, enslave its populace, inspect every child born until I find that mark. Then the ritual will proceed, Nagash will have his prize and I my final victory. As soon as the Realmgate is reopened I will send word to attack – and here is the one who will carry it.'

She pointed and Kaspar caught sight

of something silver, flickering in the darkness. They'd ridden off the main track, approaching the edge of a deep black pit dug into the rock. Inside it Kaspar saw movement and heard the rattle of a chain.

'General Bloodspeed,' Ashnakh said. 'Are you ready to ride on my command?'

There was another liquid flash and suddenly a figure stood beside them, smiling coldly. The soulblight vampire was slender and long-limbed, standing eye to eye with Kaspar on horseback. His lightweight

armour had been fashioned from beaten silver, carved with ancient symbols that seemed to shift beneath Kaspar's gaze. But even more remarkable was the swiftness with which he moved. Moments ago he'd been on the far side of the large pit; now he was right beside them, inspecting Kaspar with a chilly stare. Before he knew it the vampire had taken hold of his hand, clasping it in his clammy grip.

'Welcome. I heard the mistress had a new... guest.' He turned Kaspar's wrist, inspecting the black mark. 'So it's true. You bear the same symbol.' A blue vein pulsed beneath the skin and the soulblight stared at it, transfixed. Kaspar tugged his hand away and Ashnakh laughed.

'Forgive the general,' she said. 'He hasn't seen a living boy in quite some time. And to answer your question, Bloodspeed, Kaspar and I share the same symbol. So you are to extend him the same courtesy, the same honour, as you would give me.'

Bloodspeed's eyes flashed, but he nodded nonetheless. 'As you wish, mistress. My steed is saddled and ready. As soon as the gate is clear I will carry word to your forces at Lifestone.'

He darted to the edge of the pit, unhooked a lantern from a post and held it out. Ashnakh peered closer, and a smile crossed her face.

'Yes,' she said. 'It's perfect.'

Kaspar looked down, following her gaze. In the belly of the pit a steel stake had been hammered into the rock. To it was attached an iron chain, and at the other end something moved in the shadows, large and scaly and made of black bones.

'My terrorgheist is hungry,' said Bloodspeed. He smiled as the creature spread its dark wings, snapping at the air as though the light from the lantern angered it. 'But that will only make her swifter. Soon we will both feed on the blood of Lifestone.'

Ashnakh laughed again, a cold, delighted sound. 'Nothing can save the city now.'

She reached for Kaspar, squeezing his shoulder until he almost cried out. 'And you will be right there by my side,' she said, lowering her voice and gazing towards the purple gleam on the horizon. 'Kaspar, we are not just bonded by the pyramid I gave you. The birthmark we bear has a strength of its own, and it is this that makes us alike. Of course, all the realm marks are powerful, as your friends have discovered. But the mark of Shyish is unique – its power is that of death, the greatest force in existence.'

'Is it... dangerous?' Kaspar asked uncertainly.

Ashnakh nodded. 'Very. But the rewards are beyond anything you can imagine. Nagash chose me because I bear his mark, because I already had his power inside me. I chose you for the same reason. I meant it when I said the Castle of Mirrors was to be your home, Kaspar. I do not know how long it will be before the next mark arises, but I want you here with me until it does. I want you to study, as I did, to learn all I have to teach you. I want you to be my apprentice.'

Darkwing squawked, flapping its wings irritably. But Kaspar forced a proud smile onto his face. 'Mistress, I couldn't imagine a greater honour, I never dreamed...'

'I have been alone here for too long,' Ashnakh went on. 'I need someone to absorb my knowledge, to share my domain, to avenge my losses and revel in my triumphs. We'll start tonight, once you're fully rested. I have so much to teach you.'

Kaspar gritted his teeth. 'That's wonderful. Truly. I just... I wanted to...'

A flicker of annoyance crossed Ashnakh's face. 'What is it? Speak your mind.'

'Well, I wondered... what happened to the *Arbour Seed*? The airship, I mean.' He spoke slowly, watching her expression.

Ashnakh frowned. 'That flying deathtrap? Why do you care?'

Kaspar shook his head. 'Oh, I don't care about the ship itself. It's just that I left something on board. My... my lock-picks,' he lied, feeling them nestled under his robe. 'They're... well I suppose they're all I have left of my old life.'

Ashnakh snorted dismissively. 'All the more reason to leave them where they are. One of the first things you'll learn is to rid yourself of sentimental attachments. You must throw away anything that reminds you of the boy you used to be.'

Kaspar pursed his lips, nodding once. There'd be another way.

'Yes, my mistress,' he muttered.

CHAPTER FIVE

The Trophy Room

The ancient war wagon lay in the bed of a stony ravine between tall panes of broken glass. The fog coiled around its wooden walls, and on the steel-plated door a series of runes had been roughly carved. Vertigan approached, tracing the runes with his fingers. Kiri felt a change in the air as though a barrier had lifted.

'Was that some kind of ward?' she asked, shifting Thanis's weight. 'Did you make these marks?'

Vertigan glanced back. 'Ghosts don't ask questions,' he said, then he yanked the door open and ducked into the belly of the carriage.

Elio looked fearfully at Kiri. 'What if he's totally lost his mind? What if he never comes back, or–'

'Don't,' Kiri told him. 'He'll be fine. He has to be. Now come on, I think she's starting to wake up.'

She carried Thanis inside, laying her down on a hard wooden bench. The door closed behind them and Kiri felt that shimmer in the air again as Vertigan's warding charm sealed them in. There was little space inside the wagon, forcing them to huddle together. Alish shivered and Elio put an arm around her shoulders.

Kiri reached for Vertigan, placing a hand on his arm. His skin was cold and clammy, his darting eyes sunken in his haggard face. At her touch he shrank back, eyeing her suspiciously.

'The frightful touch,' he muttered. 'Dreadful, dreadful.'

'The nighthaunts did this,' Kiri realised. 'They must have surrounded him. He would have tried to fight them off, but there were too many.'

'It's the worst thing in the world,' a voice said, and Kiri turned. Thanis was struggling up, her face pale in the dim light. 'The fear, it's... it's unimaginable.'

'The fear,' Vertigan agreed quietly.

'What about our marks?' Alish asked. 'We could try and give Vertigan some of our strength, couldn't we? See if that might bring him back.'

'He doesn't even want me to touch him,' Kiri said. 'I think it'll take more than that.'

'What's he been living on?' Elio asked. 'He's been here a week, what's he been doing for food and water?'

At this Vertigan reached above his head, lifting down a metal bucket that hung from a hook. He dug inside, scooping out a handful of something squelchy and grey. It looked like moss but it had clearly been dead for some time, turned dark and rotten. Vertigan raised his fist and squeezed, and a trickle of foul brown water leaked

into his open mouth. Then he stuffed
the moss in as well, chewing and
swallowing as the others watched in
disgust. He held out the bucket but
Elio shook his head.

'Maybe later.'

'So what are we supposed to do?'
Thanis asked. 'Just stay in here eating
dead moss until Ashnakh needs us
again?'

'It'll be a squeeze,' Alish said, looking
around.

'Cosy, though,' Elio pointed out.

'I saw something,' Kiri told them. 'Off
in the distance, when the tree burned.
A purple light. At first I wasn't sure,
but thinking about it, it makes sense.
That army of Ashnakh's came through
the Realmgate to Ghyran, right? But
where did they come *from*? I think the
other end of the gate is here. I think I
saw it.'

'So you're saying if we could make
it to the gate, it'd take us home?' Elio
said.

Kiri nodded. The word had never sounded so sweet. 'It's not going to be easy,' she cautioned. 'First we have to find a way out of this accursed labyrinth. Then we have to sneak up to the gate without getting caught.'

'We also have to hope Ashnakh has been able to open it again after we flooded it,' Thanis pointed out.

'And before we can do any of that, we have to find Kaspar,' Alish said, and they all turned to look at her. 'I mean, we're not just going to leave him here, are we?'

Thanis frowned. 'He lied to us, Alish. He betrayed me, his best friend.'

'He's on Ashnakh's side now,' Elio agreed. 'If by some miracle we managed to find him, he'd just call her and she'd stick us right back in here.'

'So we're not even going to try?' Alish asked. 'We're just going to abandon him?' She looked pleadingly at Kiri. 'You must agree with me. Kaspar's one of us.'

Kiri opened her mouth but no words came. Alish was right, Kaspar was part of their family. But he'd also torn that family apart.

'Wh... whatever,' a voice murmured and Kiri saw Vertigan leaning forward, his hands clasped. 'Whatever happens, st... stay together. We'll come through this.'

Kiri knew those words, she'd heard them before. They'd been among Vertigan's last words to her, before the Skaven had raided the Arbour and

stolen him away. He looked up and his eyes were moist, a faint, perplexed smile playing over his lips. 'Stay together,' he repeated, and Kiri nodded.

'Well,' she said quietly. 'That decides it. We're going after Kaspar.'

Throwing down his fork, Kaspar looked in disgust at the food piled in front of him. It looked mouth-watering enough – slices of roast rhinox, fried tubers and wilted greens, frosted cakes and sugar-laced delicacies. But it all tasted the same – like earth and ash.

He crossed to the outer wall of his chamber, looking down between the drifting mirrors. Mist coiled at the base of the tower, the labyrinth stretching away into it on every side. He wondered how Thanis was doing – had she figured out a way to punch a nighthaunt yet? Kiri would be searching for an escape route, and Alish would be thinking up some clever way to ward off the spectres. Elio would be complaining, of course, but he'd be holding the others together too.

'We can help you find your friends,' a voice said, and Kaspar spun. In the nearest mirror the ghost children gradually appeared, their faces pale beneath the glass. 'We know the paths through the labyrinth. We've been there.'

Kaspar hesitated, then shook his head. 'They're not my friends any more. They wouldn't want to see me.'

'Then let us help you in other ways,' the blue girl offered. 'There must be something you need.'

Kaspar looked at her cautiously, then he came to a decision. 'The airship,' he said. 'The *Arbour Seed*. If you take me to it, I'll hear you out.'

The children whispered together, then the pale boy turned back to address Kaspar. 'It won't be easy, but we can take you. Then you must promise to listen to us, and help us if you can.'

Kaspar nodded, unhooking the pyramid pendant and placing it on the table. 'But if this is some kind of trick...'

'It's not,' the black-haired girl said. 'Trust us, Kaspar.'

They led him back along the mirrored corridors to the spiral stairway with its terrible column of bones. He could still feel those waves of mystical power radiating from inside, pulsating invisibly. The children led him upwards, drifting through the mirrors, following the course of the stairway. Up and up they climbed, the steps winding around the inner circumference of the castle. Passages opened on either side, glass corridors leading to constantly changing rooms. He saw misted spectres coiled in pools of limpid light, dim figures straining at vast mirrored machines, more bones arranged in the forms of clocks and engines and even musical instruments. He heard a dark but melodious chime sounding through the air. He knew that song. He'd dreamed it.

The children beckoned him on, climbing and climbing until the air grew thin. 'It's in here,' the blue girl said as they reached the top and Kaspar paused to catch his breath. 'Behind these walls is Ashnakh's trophy room.'

Kaspar looked up and his heart sank. 'Great. And how am I meant to get to it?'

In front of him was another wall of mirrors, circling in the peak of the castle. But these weren't floating slowly like the ones below – this high up the walls moved in rapid succession, like blades whipping through the air. And that wasn't the worst of it – beyond the first mirrored barrier was another, and beyond that a third. Every so often the gaps between the mirrors would line up and he could see into the room beyond – a domed hall filled with silent, gleaming objects. But how could he possibly reach them?

He gritted his teeth. He'd been a thief

his whole life – if anyone was made for this, he was. Between each of the mirrored walls was a gap just wide enough for him to perch in, if he stood bolt upright. He could take the barriers one by one.

He balled his fists, knowing he had to time it just right. The mirrors whipped past, their edges sharp and shining. The ghost children watched in silence – if they had breath to hold, Kaspar thought to himself, they'd have held it.

He counted to three, and jumped.

He felt the wind of the mirror as it sliced behind him, and glancing back he saw a few strands of his hair swirling in the breeze. He tucked in his stomach, the sound of the mirrors thrumming in his ears. He gauged the speed of the second barrier, counting on his fingers. Then he stepped forward, pulling up short and balancing on his tiptoes.

He could see the space beyond more clearly now, enough to see that it wasn't so much a room as a kind of platform, a circle of shadeglass perched on the very tip of the castle. Mirrors floated overhead, forming a dome of crystalline light through which bright sunlight slanted.

The barrier ahead of him was moving faster than the others, whipping through the air like thrown knives. He bit his lip, trying to work up the courage, knowing that if he slipped he could lose a finger, a foot, a hand.

But he had no choice. If the *Arbour Seed* was in there, he had to find it. And its precious cargo.

He watched the mirrors whirling past, timed to the beat of his thumping heart.

Then he leapt.

He was almost through when the mirror struck him, spinning him off his feet and onto the smooth glass floor. He rolled, trying not to cry out, coming to rest on his back. He felt a stab of pain and jerked his leg up, bracing for the worst.

The back of his shoe had been

sheared clean off, and through it he could see his own heel, the skin sliced so thinly that just a trickle of blood had leaked out. He let out a breath and climbed unsteadily to his feet.

'That was amazing,' the pale boy said and Kaspar started, looking around. At first he couldn't see the spectral children, then his eyes dropped and he realised they were floating within the shadeglass floor, drifting face up like swimmers under ice. 'Some of us thought you'd never make it. We're glad you're still in one piece.'

Kaspar nodded shakily. 'So am I.' Past the children he could see down to the spiral staircase, descending into the castle. With an effort of will he tore his eyes away, scanning the trophy room.

The domed space was filled with objects and artefacts, arranged haphazardly everywhere he looked. As he picked his way through he saw the battered helmet of a Fyreslayer chieftain, and the twin battle-lances of an Aelven princeling. He saw golden goblets and tattered, bloodstained banners, filigreed jewellery and velvet robes. On a raised plinth lay a splintered sword, beside a ruby-red helmet that could only have come from a Stormcast Eternal. A broken staff was topped with a pulsating black stone, floating above a transparent casket heaped with grimy skulls.

'They are mementoes of Ashnakh's victories,' the tall boy said, drifting beneath Kaspar's feet, pulling himself along with flattened palms. 'All the battles she has won for the Lord Nagash.'

'She likes to look at them,' the black-haired girl added. 'They remind her of her own power. And others' weakness.'

Kaspar moved through the forest of trophies and display cases, ducking beneath the suspended skull and spine of a giant fire-wyrm. Then he saw something on the far side and circled towards it, his heart thumping.

The *Arbour Seed* floated upright, suspended by an invisible force. The Kharadron aether-endrin rose over the open belly of the airship and the hull was splintered in quite a few places, but still the sight of it brought tears to Kaspar's eyes.

Beside the airship a crystal case hung in the air, and inside it he could see more tokens of Ashnakh's victory over his companions – Kiri's catapult, Alish's hammer and the staff Thanis had carried, the one that had belonged to Vertigan. He placed his hand on the case for a moment, then he crossed to the airship and peered inside.

At first all he could see were shadows. There was a discarded boot in the belly of the ship and the empty cloth sack that had once held Torvald Skysplitter's gift of aether-gold.

'Hello?' he whispered, hoping beyond hope. 'Are you here?'

Silence descended, and for a moment

all he could hear was the hum of the rotating mirrors and the distant roar of the ocean. Then there was a shout and something leapt from under the far bench, a tiny figure that sprang across the airship, launched itself into the air and took hold of Kaspar by his collar. He felt arms around his neck, squeezing so tight he began to choke.

'Yes, it's me,' he said. 'I'm happy to see you too, Scratch.'

The ragged boy pulled back, grinning through cracked teeth. He looked even

scrawnier than the last time Kaspar
had seen him, hunched at the railing
of the black ship. His mind went back
to the moment when they'd faced each
other, the boy's face a mask of absolute
terror. In a flash Kaspar had known
what to do, how to trick Ashnakh, how
to postpone her plans and save his
friends.

Speaking as quietly and as quickly
as he could he'd begged Scratch to
trust him, to listen to his words and
remember every one. Then he'd urged
him to jump – to jump, but not to fall.
He should find a place to hide, then
when night came he should return to
the airship and wait there for Kaspar.

He'd watched, heart-in-mouth, as
Scratch had flung himself over the
railing, grabbing a loose rope as he
fell and swinging back into the ship
through an open porthole. Kaspar had
cried out, fixing an expression of horror
on his face. Then he had turned and
lied to Ashnakh, his heart pounding as

her cries of frustrated rage filled the air.

'I'm sorry it took me so long to come back for you,' he told Scratch now, rubbing his filthy head. 'On the boat she was always watching me, and then I didn't know what she'd done with the *Arbour Seed*.' He fumbled in his pocket, pulling out a hunk of bread and a slab of meat. 'It tastes terrible, but it'll keep you going.'

Scratch tucked in eagerly and Kaspar leaned on the side of the airship. 'I've been trying to think of a plan to get us all out of here but it's complicated, there's a Realmgate and a silver vampire and the others are stuck in this terrible labyrinth.'

Scratch pointed at Kaspar's chest, miming the shape of the pyramid. 'Right, that's how she was keeping an eye on us. I've taken it off so she doesn't know what I'm up to, but it won't be long before she notices. For now I think it's best if you stay up here. I'll bring more food when I can, and I'll let you know when I've figured out how to rescue Thanis and everyone.'

'We said we can take you to them, if you'll help us.'

The ghost children floated through the glass under their feet and Scratch leapt into the air, perching on the airship's railing and shaking uncontrollably.

'It's okay,' Kaspar said soothingly. 'They're friends. At least, I think they are.' He peered down. 'Let's say I agreed to help. What would you want me to do?'

'This way,' the blue girl said. 'We'll show you.'

She beckoned towards the centre of the circle, and for the first time Kaspar noticed that the glass platform wasn't complete. There was a perfectly round hole in the middle of the floor, and from it a livid, swirling glow was rising.

He approached it, moving cautiously. Scratch tugged his sleeve but Kaspar shook him off.

'It's okay, I'll be careful.'

He steeled himself, crossing towards the hole. Whatever was down there was silent but somehow he could still hear it, like a roaring in his head. It seemed to pull at him, invisible tendrils tugging at his nerves, his mind, his soul. He stepped to the edge and looked down.

A bolt of pain shot through his head but he managed to hold his gaze for a few seconds, his mind struggling to process what he'd seen. It looked like a whirlpool, a maelstrom of mystical energy enclosed by the column of bones around which the entire Castle of Mirrors revolved. Spectres moved in the current, and he heard the distant wail of wandering souls.

He staggered back, clasping a hand to his forehead. 'What is it? It's hideous.'

'It is called the Vortex of Sundered Spirits,' the tall boy said. 'Created from the shattered souls of all those who died on the Battlerock in a century of conflict.'

'Ashnakh bound them to her will,' the blue girl went on. 'She used them to create this castle, to power the labyrinth. Then she used their bones to wall the vortex in.'

'It must be destroyed,' the pale boy whispered. 'If the vortex were unbalanced, her castle would crumble, and we would be set free.'

Kaspar looked at them in amazement. 'You want me to destroy a mystical vortex? What do you think I am, some kind of wizard?'

'You're alive,' the first boy insisted. 'Life can defeat death.'

Kaspar threw up his hands. 'I'm just a common street thief, I don't know anything about magical whirlpools or sundered spirits.'

The pale girl sighed. 'You won't even try. You won't help us, that crazy old man wouldn't help us...'

Kaspar looked at her in surprise. 'What crazy old man?'

'The one in the labyrinth,' the pale

boy explained. 'We asked him first, but he just yelled at us. Told us we were figments of his imagination.'

'There was something about him, though,' the black-haired girl mused. 'Something... familiar.'

'Vertigan,' Kaspar whispered, hoping beyond hope. 'It has to be. She's been keeping him in the labyrinth, just like the others. I don't know why he wouldn't help you, but if anyone would know about vortexes and stuff, it's him. You have to take me to him.'

A sudden sound pierced the silence, somewhere outside the revolving dome. Kaspar gestured to Scratch and the boy ducked back, cowering behind a giant six-tusked skull. The ghost children vanished, dissipating into the mirrors as an irritable caw rang out and a black shape descended into the trophy room.

Darkwing landed on Kaspar's shoulder, fixing him with a hard, accusing stare. Around its neck the raven bore the pyramid pendant, the weight forcing its head down. Kaspar unhooked it and the bird gave a croak of dismay.

'The time must've got away from me,' Kaspar said, placing it hurriedly around his neck. 'She's probably expecting me for our first lesson. I'm to be the mistress's apprentice, it's a great honour.'

The bird bobbed its head, croaking drily. Then it gave Kaspar a peck behind the ear, sharp and vicious, and jerked its head towards the stairs.

'Hey,' he protested. 'I'm going, all right? You horrible little creature.'

CHAPTER SIX

The Sorceress's Apprentice

Ashnakh was waiting for him in a long
corridor near the base of the castle,
her face dark with suspicion. Darkwing
flapped down and perched on her
shoulder, chattering in her ear.

'Mistress, my apologies,' Kaspar began.
'I was exploring this wondrous castle
and I simply lost track of—'

He gasped as he felt his feet leave
the ground, his body tipping forward
until he hung face down, suspended
above the mirrored floor. Ashnakh made
a gesture and his arms flew outward,

stretching until he heard the joints in his elbows creak. His legs did the same, yanked backwards like there were ropes around his ankles, tugging him in every direction at once. His fingers strained, his shoulders popped, and he knew that if she wanted to Ashnakh could tear him limb from limb.

'It's my own fault,' she hissed, regarding him with cold, unsympathetic eyes. 'I forgot who you were. To most children, a barrier like the one around my trophy room would be a warning. To a thief like you, it's an invitation.'

She waved a hand and Kaspar dropped, crashing face down.

'From now on you keep that pendant around your neck at all times,' the sorceress told him. 'I'll know if you take if off.'

Kaspar staggered to his feet. 'Yes, mistress,' he managed.

Ashnakh's expression softened. 'There's no harm in being inquisitive,' she said. 'I was, at your age. But you must respect the boundaries placed upon you, or be prepared to face the consequences. Now come, it's time to begin your training.'

She led him along the wide, downward-sloping corridor into the echoing under-chambers of the castle. The arched walls were patterned with a mirrored mosaic, their reflections cut and splintered into a thousand shimmering shapes – he saw mouths, eyes, towers and monsters. At the end was a huge glass doorway made from two opposing panels, and in each one Kaspar could see spectres moving, shapes writhing in the tinted glass. Guardians, protecting whatever was inside.

Ashnakh spoke a string of dark words and the ghastly forms withdrew, the vast doors swinging silently open. 'This is the place where I learned who I truly am,' she said, beckoning Kaspar forward. 'This is where I became Ashnakh.'

The hall was impossibly massive, its far walls and its mirrored ceiling lost in fog. But it was not dark or gloomy, it was a place of shimmering, spectral light, shafts and sparks illuminating every corner. Kaspar couldn't make out the source of the light but he could see it reflected in a thousand pieces of shadeglass, all of them floating untethered through the grand space.

Then he saw that these weren't simple panes like the ones surrounding the castle. They were containers and

caskets, chests and coffers, racks and shelves all fashioned from translucent materials. And inside and upon them were heaped every kind of mystical artefact Kaspar could imagine – cauldrons and alembics, scales and divining wands, staffs of wood and bone and steel. There were books, too – rows of leather-bound tomes, stacks of scrolls and parchments, all floating silently through the luminous air. High up, near the ceiling, he saw a cluster of crates all chained together, shuddering and clattering as though something big and angry were trapped inside.

'When Lord Nagash brought me back, he taught me many things.' The sorceress strode across the smooth glass floor, weaving between a pair of low-flying strongboxes. 'But it was here, in this castle I created myself, that I learned the full extent of my power. In harnessing the forces of death that haunt the Battlerock I was able to confront and control the darkness that was always inside me. Soon you will, too.'

They passed a line of high-sided cabinets drifting close to the ground, each one containing the bleached skeleton of a different creature – a dire wolf, a Duardin, an Orruk, a man. Something lashed at Kaspar and he jumped, remembering the vines that had attacked them in the ancient forest. He found himself staring into the petalled mouth of a huge dead plant that lolled from an open-topped chest, its stem and roots turned grey, its zombie flowers coughing ash-coloured pollen.

He backed away as the vines reached for him. And as he did so he saw something gleaming overhead, a golden light that contrasted with the silver shine all around. He knew that light; he recognised it right away. He felt his pulse quicken.

'Don't dawdle,' Ashnakh said over her shoulder. 'There are a thousand ways to die in here.'

Kaspar gulped, hurrying after her. 'That won't be... necessary, will it?' he asked. 'I won't have to actually die to be your apprentice?'

The sorceress smiled coldly. 'No. But the process will change you in ways you cannot predict. As I told you, the power we bear is great, but it exacts a toll.'

Kaspar swallowed. That wasn't a very comforting answer.

They had reached an open space in the middle of the hall, where the floor was covered in a layer of clinging mist. Racks and caskets drifted in a circular motion, and in the centre was a mirrored dais. Upon it stood a large wooden box – a coffin, Kaspar realised. Darkwing circled overhead, coming to rest on a high shelf with its wings folded.

Ashnakh crossed to the coffin and stood over it, her hands aloft. Kaspar waited on the edge of the circle, watching as the mist began to twist and coil, rising in slender strands. Ashnakh whispered under her breath, dark syllables that seemed to overlap discordantly as though several voices were speaking at once. On her wrist Kaspar saw the rune of Shyish glowing, and he felt his own mark tingle in response.

The coffin began to tremble, rattling on the plinth. From inside a dark smoke was rising, twining with the pale mist. Ashnakh's words grew more insistent; she seemed to be calling, summoning something to her. Kaspar's blood was like ice but he forced himself to keep watching.

Then there was a piercing scream from inside the coffin, a raw, hideous sound that scraped on Kaspar's ears. Ashnakh reached out, beckoning.

'That's good,' she said. 'Come, my servant. Rise.'

A dark shape emerged from the coffin, hooded in black smoke, its bone-white face formed from coils of mist, hardening as Kaspar watched. The nighthaunt let out another screech as Ashnakh's fingers coiled in the air, drawing it up into the light.

'This will be one of the first things I'll teach you,' the sorceress said, glancing back at Kaspar. 'You'll learn how to summon them, and how to control them.'

She raised her wrist, turning her birthmark towards the nighthaunt. It saw the rune and shied away, hissing. Ashnakh advanced, backing the phantom towards Kaspar. He stepped away hurriedly; he didn't want that foul thing anywhere near him.

'Don't be a coward,' Ashnakh said. 'Command it. Use your mark.'

On Kaspar's wrist the rune was tingling, ringed with a faint red glow. He held it up and suddenly he felt a wave of power coursing through him. But it wasn't the same power he'd shared with the others – it was harder, somehow; sharper, icier.

The nighthaunt looked from Kaspar to Ashnakh, its chains shivering. Kaspar took a step forward, driving the phantom back. The power rushed to his head, a rich, enveloping blackness flooding his senses. He could smell rot and damp earth but somehow it was sweet to him, the scent of ageless decay and infinite possibility. *So this is why she does it*, he thought. *This is why she embraces the dark.*

The nighthaunt withdrew and Kaspar

advanced, giddy with the sensation rushing through him. He could hear Ashnakh whispering encouragingly.

'That's right, control it. Bend it to your will.'

Kaspar smiled, and a vision flashed into his mind – of him learning everything Ashnakh had to teach, growing his strength until it rivalled her own then turning it against her. Yes, his friends might have to suffer a little, but it would be worth it in the end. If he was as strong as Ashnakh he could keep them safe forever; he could save Lifestone, perhaps even be crowned lord...

There was a sudden crash and Darkwing took to the air, squawking. Kaspar felt his power falter, the nighthaunt fleeing into the sparkling gloom. He staggered, suddenly weak, as though something had been torn from inside him.

'What was that?' Ashnakh demanded, turning furiously. Across the hall

Kaspar could see the great doors standing open, a silver shape darting towards them. Then without warning Bloodspeed was standing there, saluting proudly.

'General,' Ashnakh said. 'Why do you disturb my lesson?'

'We're through,' the soulblight said, his fangs glistening. 'The gate is open, my mistress. All we need to do is clear out the rubble and we'll be ready to march.'

Ashnakh hissed with delight. 'That is very good news,' she said. 'Gather the troops. And saddle your steed, as soon as the way is clear I want you to carry word to our armies at Lifestone. Tell them to start the assault. I will follow as swiftly as I can.'

Kaspar looked up at her. 'Wh-what should I do?'

Ashnakh barely glanced at him. 'Go to your room. Await my orders.' And she marched towards the doors, Bloodspeed at her side and Darkwing circling overhead.

Kaspar was left alone in the centre of the hall, his breath loud in the stillness. The terrible power had receded, leaving him drained and unsteady. But he could still recall how it had felt, how invincible he'd been, how superior to everything and everyone. He wanted badly to feel that way again, but he knew how dangerous it could be.

He shook himself, making for the doors. Bloodspeed had said the Realmgate was open, their army could pass through. Which meant that Kaspar had run out of time – he had to find Vertigan and the others, and he had to do it now.

Then that golden shimmer caught his eye again and he paused, peering up. There was a glass container drifting overhead, heaped with flasks and jars filled with strange, unquiet substances. But the aether-gold shone brighter than the rest, seeming to call to Kaspar as he jumped up and snatched at it, slipping the flask into his pocket.

He stepped out into the hallway, looking up at the mirrors that arched overhead.

'Hey,' he called out. 'Where are you? I need your help, and I need it now.'

CHAPTER SEVEN

The Lost Children

The abyss stretched ahead of them,
cutting through the Shatterglass
Labyrinth like a jagged wound. Peering
over the edge Elio could see nothing –
no bottom, and no way to climb down.
On the far side the Castle of Mirrors
rose from the fog, shimmering as the
sun touched the horizon and night
came to reclaim the Battlerock.

He let go of Kiri's wrist and the
connection between them broke. It felt
like days since they'd left the safety of
Vertigan's armoured wagon and set out
into the labyrinth, though Elio knew it
was merely hours. They'd been hoping

their marks would lead them to Kaspar, but it didn't seem to be working – every time they got closer to the castle, it seemed to move away. Ashnakh had placed spells on the labyrinth to misguide and bewilder her prisoners; perhaps they confused the birthmarks, too.

And now this great chasm had appeared, blocking their way. Behind them he could hear wails in the fog as the nighthaunts circled. Alish shivered, drawing closer to Thanis. Vertigan stood behind them, his jaw slack and his eyes unfocused. *He should be leading us*, Elio thought. *Instead he's even more helpless than we are.*

'Look,' Kiri said, pointing. A last shaft of sunlight had pierced the fog, reflected from the peak of the castle, and in its glow Elio saw a rising shape on the edge of the abyss. 'Is that a bridge?'

'I think so,' he nodded. 'Let's take a look.'

They hurried towards it, the mist

breaking and reforming around them. Soon the shape had coalesced into a black structure, a single span of smooth stone reaching like an outstretched arm to the far side of the chasm. It was narrow, just wide enough to walk across, and there was no lip or railing. But what choice did they have?

'I'll cross first,' Kiri said. 'Make sure it'll definitely hold us. Alish, you next, then Elio with Vertigan. Thanis can bring up the rear.'

The tall girl nodded. 'Let's just hope those things don't find us before we're safely across.'

Kiri stepped onto the bridge, testing each step. The mist closed around her and she was soon lost from view. 'It seems solid,' her disembodied voice called back. 'Alish, come after me. Don't wait.'

Alish nodded, holding her arms out for balance as she crossed. Elio approached the bridge, feeling his heart tighten. Yes, he'd grown a lot braver in the past few days, especially since the Sylvaneth had healed him. But the thought of tiptoeing across a narrow span above an unfathomable abyss was still enough to put the fear in him. Almost as much as those hideous–

The nighthaunt screamed right behind them and he jerked round, eyes wide.

'Go,' Thanis said. 'Right now.'

Elio took hold of Vertigan's arm, leading him forward. The bridge rose into the fog and he stepped onto it, feeling the old man's hand trembling in his grasp.

'Just follow me,' he said, wondering if Vertigan even understood him. 'We'll make it across, you'll see.'

There was another scream in the fog, but now he couldn't tell where it was coming from – ahead or behind? He heard a shout, strong and defiant, but it could have been either Kiri or Thanis. Glancing down he saw the darkness opening up below him, the chasm seeming to beckon him in. Hurriedly he looked away.

He reached the peak of the span and started to descend, leading Vertigan with cautious steps. The shouts continued, muffled and indistinct. Then a dark shape appeared behind him, seeming to float through the air. He grabbed Vertigan, trying to pull him forward, but the old man stumbled and almost slipped. Elio was driven sideways, teetering on the edge of the bridge, clutching at Vertigan's arm.

Then his master suddenly steadied, as someone pulled him back. It was

Thanis, yanking Vertigan to safety and Elio along with him.

'Go!' she shouted. 'They're right behind me.'

Chains clattered in the mist and Elio ran as the nighthaunts pursued them across the bridge. He could see the other side now, a darkness more solid than the gulf below, and as he hurried towards it he saw Kiri and Alish standing with their backs to him. More nighthaunts surrounded them, forcing them back. Elio cursed silently. So there were phantoms behind them, and ahead as well. They were trapped.

He jumped down from the bridge as the spirits circled in, cackling and rattling. Vertigan and Thanis joined him and the five of them huddled together, facing out into the fog. A row of misshapen mirrors rose ahead of Elio, splintered glass fragments rising like standing stones. The nighthaunts drifted between them, one clutching a long, notched sword, black smoke writhing around the blade.

'Get back, you fiends,' Elio said, but his voice was weak and his words got lost.

Alish cried out as a nighthaunt lunged, arms outstretched. She ducked instinctively and Elio saw its bony fingers scrape across Vertigan's skin. The old man fell with a cry, dropping in the dirt. The nighthaunts cackled gleefully.

Then he heard something up ahead – a voice, and footsteps. The fog swirled and there was a cry of 'Begone!' The nighthaunts seemed to hesitate, turning as a hooded figure bounded between the mirrors. He held up an arm, a dark rune glowing on his skin.

'Begone! I command it!'

The phantoms withdrew, shrinking from the blazing mark. Elio took a step forward as Kaspar threw back his hood, his eyes flashing. In that moment he seemed taller somehow, stern and powerful.

The nighthaunts fled, their shrieks
fading into the distance. Elio helped
Vertigan to his feet as Kaspar
approached.

'Master Vertigan,' Kaspar said
breathlessly. 'It is you.'

Kiri stepped forward, raising her fists.
'That's close enough,' she told Kaspar.

In a heartbeat his expression changed,
from hope to outright anger. 'I just
saved your life,' he said bitterly. 'Want
me to call those things back? I can,
you know.'

Thanis faced him. 'What are you doing here, Kaspar? Did you send the nighthaunts away so you could gloat over us in peace?'

Kaspar's mouth twisted. 'Don't you dare–'

Vertigan stepped between them, holding up a trembling hand. 'Together,' he whispered hoarsely. 'Stay *together*.'

Kaspar looked at the old man and suddenly his anger abated, the darkness that had come over him seeming to drain away. 'What *happened* to him?' he asked.

'Your mistress happened,' Thanis growled. 'Your precious Ashnakh. She left him in the labyrinth and those nighthaunts came for him.'

Kaspar sighed. 'I'm sorry. I guess it's time I explained what's been going on.'

'We don't care,' Thanis said. 'We don't care what you have to say.'

Kaspar looked at her pleadingly. 'But I really did come to rescue you!'

'You expect us to believe that?' Elio

demanded. 'After you left us in that box for days, to rot?'

'You let Scratch die,' Alish said tearfully. 'You just stood there and watched.'

'Scratch is alive!' Kaspar cried. 'I swear. He's waiting with the *Arbour Seed* so we can all get out of here.'

'Why should we believe you?' Thanis demanded. 'She probably sent you, to give us false hope.'

'I never had a choice,' Kaspar insisted. 'She was so powerful, I knew it right from the start. She spoke to me through the pyramid, told me if I did as she asked, if I let her watch everything that happened, then I'd get to see Master Vertigan again. And look, it's true.'

'So you were spying on us all along?' Kiri asked.

'I had to make her trust me,' Kaspar explained. 'It was the only way, you must see that. But now there's no more time, she's opened the Realmgate, she's going to attack Lifestone. We have to go while she's distracted.' He reached into his pocket, drawing out the flask of aether-gold. 'Look, I stole this from her supplies. If we can make it to the airship it should be enough to fly us home.'

'We can't trust you,' Thanis said. 'You lied to us. To *me*.'

'I know,' Kaspar pleaded. 'I never knew when she was watching, or listening. The only safe place was inside my head.'

'Quiet.' Kiri held up a hand, looking around. The mirrors glittered and Elio saw Vertigan staring into one of them, frowning as something moved in the shadows.

'It's all right,' Kaspar said. 'They're my friends.'

Elio was amazed to see figures in the mirrors, misty forms beneath the glass. They darkened as they drew nearer, five ghostly children peering out cautiously.

'Their spirits were trapped by Ashnakh,' Kaspar explained. 'They helped me find you.'

'Who are they?' Elio asked. A girl stared back at him, her eyes a misty blue.

'I don't know,' Kaspar admitted. 'They've been here so long they've forgotten their own names.'

'Ryla,' Vertigan said and the ghost children looked at him in surprise. 'Gethris,' he said, pointing at the tall boy in the centre. 'Samkin. Kether. Sali. I know them.'

The boy, Gethris, screwed up his face as though trying to remember. 'M-Mikal?'

Vertigan smiled, and as Elio watched his eyes seemed to regain some of their focus. 'You came before, didn't you? But I was lost in fear. Ah, it has been so long. So long since she tore us apart.'

'They were your chosen,' Kiri realised aloud. 'The ones who bore the realm marks with you. Weren't they?'

Gethris held up his wrist and Elio saw the mark of Ghyran, matching his own. As the other ghost children did the same he saw Kiri stepping forward, and Thanis, and Alish.

'We were called to save the city,' Vertigan muttered, his cracked voice steeped in sadness. 'We were ready for the ritual. But she let the darkness in, and only I survived.' He lifted his head. 'If I had known you were trapped here, I would have...'

'You've come now, Mikal,' Gethris said. 'And Kaspar has promised that you'll help us if you can. Are you willing to try?'

Vertigan nodded, his hands shaking. 'I'm weak,' he said. 'But I'll do what I can.'

CHAPTER EIGHT

The Spiral Staircase

The ghost children led the way and the
others followed, hastening through
the labyrinth as phantoms howled
in the fog. Kaspar felt unsteady on his
feet, the after-effects of that dark power
still rattling his nerves. Ashnakh had
warned him that using it would take a
toll, and she was right. He could feel
a change deep inside himself, a kind of
emptiness, as though something vital
had been removed and not yet replaced.
But if it helped him save his friends, it
would be worth it.

Suddenly the Castle of Mirrors was
ahead of them, sheer and shimmering.

A flight of glass steps led up to its grand, arched entrance and Elio took hold of Vertigan's arm, helping him inside. They gazed up and around as they entered, marvelling at the mirrored surfaces floating around them, the grand hallway into which they hurried, their feet loud on the glass.

Then they saw the column of bones and recoiled, skidding to a halt. Only Vertigan would approach it, gazing up in disbelief as though struggling to comprehend what he was seeing.

'So many souls,' he muttered. 'I can feel them.'

'They're trapped inside,' Kaspar said, reaching the base of the staircase. 'There's a kind of vortex, but we can't get to it from here. We need to go up.' He pointed overhead and the others raised their heads, seeing the bone stairway winding above them.

'Is the *Arbour Seed* up there?' Alish asked.

Kaspar nodded. 'And Scratch too. So

let's move.'

He bounded up the stairs, Kiri and Alish on his heels. Thanis and Elio each took one of Vertigan's arms, helping him up the first flight. He kept to the far wall, away from the column of bones, unable to stop staring at it.

'So much death,' he said, almost to himself. 'Aisha, what have you done?'

'I told you, old man. It's Ashnakh now.'

Kaspar turned sharply, looking down. The sorceress stood at the base of the steps, Darkwing perched on her shoulder. Bloodspeed stood at her side, his sword unsheathed, and in the shadows behind him Kaspar saw a shuffling mob of deadwalker soldiers, their notched, rusty weapons already drawn.

Ashnakh started up the stairs and the grim host followed. Tendrils of mist coiled behind her in the shadows, pale apparitions emerging from it. Vertigan recoiled when he saw the nighthaunts, and Ashnakh's smile widened.

'I see my chainghasts have done their work,' she said. 'Honestly, Mikal, I thought you were stronger. But you're just a pathetic, tired old man.'

'You leave him alone!' Elio shouted, backing up the stairs and drawing Vertigan with him. 'He's ten times stronger than you!'

Ashnakh laughed, then she gestured to Bloodspeed. 'Bring them to me. Now.'

The soulblight sprang forward, his sword shimmering. He raised it, and behind him the hordes of the dead let out a rattling cry.

'Come on,' Kaspar yelled. 'Run!'

They sprinted up the stairway, Kiri in the lead, Alish and Kaspar close behind her. Thanis and Elio followed with Vertigan, who was staggering up the steps as fast as he could. But Ashnakh's forces were already gaining, their hideous cries pursuing them.

'I can hear your hearts beating,' Bloodspeed snarled. 'My only question is, whose blood should I taste first?'

He darted in, a blur of silver and red, and Elio cried out as the soulblight appeared at his side, seizing him with one gloved hand. Thanis dragged Vertigan clear, both of them stumbling back as Bloodspeed sniffed at Elio, his lip curling.

'This one smells like moss and branches and foul Sylvaneth,' he snarled, dropping the boy. Then his head lifted and he eyed Alish, smiling cruelly. 'How about you?' he said, exposing his fangs. 'The small ones are always the sweetest.'

'You leave her alone!' Thanis bounded between them, fear and anger fighting on her face.

'Thanis, no!' Alish cried. 'He's too quick.'

'You should listen,' Bloodspeed snarled. 'Keep running, and maybe you can escape while I'm busy with your friend.'

Thanis shook her head. 'Didn't your mistress tell you? I never run from a fight.'

She sprang down the steps, reaching
the soulblight and shoving him hard
in the chest. Kaspar could tell from
Bloodspeed's expression that he hadn't
expected her to go on the attack; he
lost his footing, stumbling back into the
mass of deadwalkers.

But he recovered himself and glared
up at Thanis, the derision in his eyes
replaced by genuine anger. 'I will kill
you for that,' he hissed, unsheathing his
sword.

'No, you won't,' Kaspar said. 'The

mistress needs us alive. Don't you?'

Ashnakh came floating up the stairway, over the heads of the corpse soldiers. She gestured to Bloodspeed and the soulblight held back, the sword shaking in his hand.

'You must have known your escape was doomed to failure,' the sorceress told Kaspar. 'You must have known I would sense what you were trying to do.'

She gestured to the pyramid around his neck and Kaspar nodded. He'd taken a calculated risk, hoping she'd be so distracted by her preparations for invasion that she wouldn't pay any attention to him. And he'd been right – up to a point.

'I could have used more time,' he admitted, stepping towards Thanis. 'But I had to try.' Glancing over his shoulder he could see the others retreating up the stairway.

Ashnakh sighed, shaking her head. 'Deep down, I always knew you'd betray me.'

Kaspar felt a smile crossing his face. 'No,' he said. 'You didn't. You think you're so powerful, but I fooled you from the start.'

Ashnakh's pale face turned even paler, her lips tightening in anger. Her hands came together and between them Kaspar saw a flicker of violet energy. Suddenly a plan formed.

'You act like you're this great sorceress,' he went on. 'But you're just a lonely old witch, hiding in your castle and plotting your revenge.'

Thanis looked at him in surprise, then she seemed to realise what Kaspar was doing and nodded forcefully. 'He's right. We flooded your Realmgate, and we escaped from your labyrinth. Admit it, you got outwitted by a bunch of kids.'

Ashnakh growled. 'When this is over, you will all pay. When the ritual is done and I have no more need of you, I will take great pleasure in your destruction.'

'And then you'll be alone again,'

Kaspar said. 'Forever and ever. How *pathetic.*'

The sorceress roared in fury, flinging her hands open in a single, vicious motion. The fire-bolt shot out, streaking towards Kaspar and Thanis. But they were ready, throwing themselves back up the stairway, leaping clear just in time. The fire-bolt struck the steps, sending shards of bone flying in all directions. Kaspar felt the force of it, spinning him off his feet and onto his knees. The stairway split apart, a wide gulf opening up. He almost stumbled into it but Thanis grabbed his hand, yanking him clear.

'Caught you again,' she said, smiling at him.

Then they heard a shout and turned. Bloodspeed teetered on the edge, struggling to maintain his balance as the stairs crumbled in front of him. He tried to retreat from the brink but the deadwalkers were still coming, driven up the steps by others pushing from behind. Kaspar could see the alarm on the soulblight's face as he realised he was falling, and there was no way to stop it.

Bloodspeed toppled over the edge with a cry of fury, spinning in mid-air and landing hard beneath them, close to the foot of the tower. Thanis peered down, giving a little wave. Then Kaspar grabbed her and they ran.

He could feel the ache in his legs as he climbed, step after step, forcing himself to keep going. Something brushed against his boots and he saw finger bones sprouting from the floor, snatching at his ankles. For a moment they tangled around his feet but he summoned his strength and yanked free, sending the bones flying loose.

Thanis was a good distance ahead of him now, and above her he could see the circular platform at the peak of the tower. They might actually have a chance.

Then he heard a shriek, and shifted

his focus. Perhaps not.

The others were gathered on an exposed landing close to the top of the tower, hemmed in together. And all around them, drifting through the very walls of the castle to pin them down, was a horde of attacking nighthaunts. Kaspar saw one of the phantoms lashing at Kiri, swiping at her clothes. Elio and Alish stood on either side of her, holding Vertigan between them, whose face was a mask of terror. Thanis reached them, darting between the spectral shapes to join her friends. Kaspar tried to hurry after her but he was exhausted, and they were so far away. All he could do was watch in horror as the phantoms circled in.

'I did warn you this would happen.'

Ashnakh rose behind him, a wicked smile on her face. 'I showed you what would transpire if you didn't do as I ordered. And now that prophecy has come to pass. Your friends will suffer, and you along with them.'

Kaspar looked at her and felt the darkness inside him, a deep well of despair threatening to open up. With an effort, he shook his head.

'Not if I have anything to do with it.'

He ran towards his friends, exposing the rune on his arm and holding it up. The nighthaunts saw it and shrieked, some of them backing away. But there were so many, and deep down he knew he wasn't strong enough to control them all.

Ashnakh laughed as her shadow fell over him. 'Pitiful,' she said as the nighthaunts tightened their cordon around his friends, reaching with their hideous, clawed hands. 'Utterly pathet–'

A yell rang out overhead, wordless and shrill, echoing in the stairwell. Something long and slender came flying through the air, cartwheeling as it fell. It was aimed towards Vertigan, and as Kaspar watched the old man gathered the last of his strength and reached up, his hand locking firmly around it.

Vertigan gripped the staff, pulling it
down and swinging it round. There
was a chorus of ghostly shrieks as
the nighthaunts tried to flee, the staff
humming as it swept through their
spectral bodies, shredding them.

There was a second shout, and
this time Kaspar saw who'd made it.
Scratch stood at the top of the stairway,
waving excitedly as he saw Alish and
Thanis and Elio. There were scrapes
on his arms and elbows, and the tip of
one ear seemed to be missing. But still

Kaspar was impressed. *The boy made it through the spinning mirrors*, he realised. *He's almost as sneaky as I am.*

Kaspar held up his wrist, throwing all of his energy into the rune. The nighthaunts shrank away and he felt the power flowing through him, revelling in it. Ashnakh bellowed in anger, preparing a fire-bolt in her hands. But Vertigan was ready – he jabbed his staff at her, waves of power radiating from the tip. Ashnakh was taken by surprise, spinning backwards through the air, the fire-bolt flying from her fingertips, bouncing off the mirrored walls.

Kaspar turned back to the retreating nighthaunts, knowing nothing could stop him now. He heard the spectres wail in fear as they darted away from him, and he jabbed his wrist at them as they fled in tatters. Jagged bolts of savage joy flooded him and he laughed, every nerve on fire.

Then a stern voice said, 'Kaspar. Stop.'

He turned furiously, raising his fist, ready to strike whoever had broken his concentration. But when he saw Vertigan looking down at him, he broke off. Suddenly the power fled and he felt a great void inside him, a terrible sense of loss.

'It's all right,' Vertigan said, holding Kaspar's shoulders in a firm grip. His eyes were clear, his expression firm. 'They're gone. You saved us.'

Kaspar looked up into his master's eyes. 'You're... you're back?' he asked. 'You're yourself again?'

Vertigan gripped the staff. 'I am. Thanks to this.'

'I brought it most of the way,' Elio put in. 'But Thanis helped.'

Thanis shot him a look, but said nothing.

'That is a dark power you possess, Kaspar,' Vertigan went on. 'The mark of Shyish exacts a toll on all those who wield it, including Aisha herself.'

'She was teaching me to control it,'

Kaspar told him. 'It drives those things away, but afterwards I feel... empty.'

Vertigan nodded. 'You must learn to understand it, to find balance within yourself. If you can, it could be a powerful weapon. Now come, let us not falter. We're almost at the top.'

They staggered up the last flight of steps, Scratch grinning at them as they approached.

'So this is the lost boy,' Vertigan said, smiling back at him. 'It's good to meet you, Scratch.'

'Thanks for saving our necks,' Kiri added, gesturing to the staff.

Kaspar faced the wall of mirrors, wondering how they were all going to make it through. But Vertigan raised his staff, muttering a few words under his breath. Kaspar saw the mirrors slowing as Vertigan exerted his will on the castle.

'Go,' he said as the walls slowed to a crawl. 'I'm still weak, it will not hold for long.'

Kaspar ducked into the trophy room, looking through the maze of artefacts to see the *Arbour Seed* floating on the far side. The others entered behind him, followed by Vertigan. The old man did look tired, Kaspar thought. But they were almost there.

'Gethris,' Vertigan said, looking down at the mirrored floor as the ghost children appeared beneath their feet. 'Show me.'

They beckoned him to the centre of the room, where the circular opening led down into the Vortex of Sundered Spirits. Kaspar could feel its power as they drew closer, and he saw Vertigan's fingers tighten around his staff as he gazed in horror.

'So much pain,' he said. 'So much death.'

'Can it be destroyed?' Kaspar asked. 'Can you break the vortex?'

Vertigan hesitated, then he nodded. 'If it were destabilised, the castle would break apart. But the vortex is a creation of death, it would take a life to disrupt it.'

'You mean...' Kaspar said in horror.

'Yes,' a voice boomed from behind them. 'Only life can defeat death.'

There was a terrible explosion, and the air was filled with flying glass.

CHAPTER NINE

The Vortex

The wall of mirrors surrounding the trophy room shattered apart, sending out a rain of shards. Kaspar shielded his face, feeling splinters in his hands and his hair. Ashnakh rose from the stairway, her hands aloft. Her face was hot with fury and her eyes flashed as she floated through the clouds of sparkling dust.

Vertigan lifted his staff, swinging it towards her, but this time Ashnakh was ready for him. A bolt of energy whipped from her hands, slamming into Vertigan and throwing him off his feet. The staff flew from his hands, clattering across

the mirrored floor. The old man landed
on his back, skidding towards the edge
of the vortex. Kiri grabbed him, hauling
him back. Vertigan tried to stand but
he was too weak.

Ashnakh laughed, her hands coiling to
form another fire-bolt. Behind her was
a wall of grey, a mass of nighthaunts
rising like a dark fog. Then suddenly
the sorceress paused, an expression
of complete surprise crossing her face.
Kaspar followed her gaze and saw
Scratch peering out from behind Thanis,
looking up nervously.

'He's alive?' Ashnakh screeched. 'All
this time?'

Kaspar nodded. 'I told you you'd been
fooled.'

'But this means the ritual is still
possible,' Ashnakh crowed. 'I can go to
Lifestone and claim my prize.'

'Not if we get there first,' Kaspar said,
and tugged the flask of aether-gold
from his pocket. He turned, pressing it
into Kiri's hand. 'Get to the airship,' he

said. 'Get Master Vertigan to safety. Be
ready to lift off.'

'No,' Thanis protested. 'We stay
together, remember?'

'Not this time,' Kaspar said. 'I'll be
right behind you, I promise.'

Kiri eyed him with concern. 'What are
you going to do?'

Kaspar smiled. 'I'm going to finish
this.'

He took a step back, and now he was
standing right on the edge of the vortex.
He watched as his friends departed, Elio
and Thanis helping Vertigan towards
the *Arbour Seed*. He was left alone with
Ashnakh and her nighthaunts.

'Let them go,' he told the sorceress.
'Or I'll tear this whole place down.'

Ashnakh glanced down at the vortex,
and her eyes narrowed. 'You wouldn't
dare. You're a thief and a coward.
You're no hero.'

'So I'm right,' Kaspar said, grinning
at her. 'Vertigan said that only life can
disrupt the vortex. I'm betting that if

I took one more step back, I could put
an end to all this. Set all the trapped
souls free, and destroy this awful castle
into the bargain.'

'You'd die,' Ashnakh told him.

'But my friends would live,' Kaspar
said. 'Of course, there is one other way
to end this.'

Ashnakh frowned. 'What is it? Speak
quickly.'

'I could stay with you,' Kaspar said.
'As your apprentice. If you let my
friends leave, if you promise never to
bother them again. If you forget about
this ritual, about Lifestone, about all of
it. We could stay together, here in this
castle, forever.'

Ashnakh started to speak but then
she broke off, looking away. When she
turned back her eyes were dark, and
he thought he saw tears in them.

'You'd do that?' she asked. 'You'd give
me your future?'

Kaspar nodded. 'Anything for my
friends.'

Then there was a screech overhead and a shadow fell over him. Kaspar looked up, shielding his face.

Darkwing swept down, its wings flapping furiously. Kaspar felt claws in his hair, the raven's beak pecking madly. He could feel the bird's hot breath, the warm blood in its body. *It's alive*, he realised suddenly. A living familiar, not a resurrected corpse like all of Ashnakh's other servants. *And life can defeat death.*

The bird pecked and cawed, striking again and again. Kaspar felt himself stumble, losing his balance.

'No!' Ashnakh shrieked. 'Darkwing, leave him!'

But it was too late. Kaspar was falling, one foot slipping over the edge, into the vortex. He could feel its power snatching at him, trying to drag him down.

Darkwing heard its mistress and broke free, untangling itself and attempting to fly away. But the power

of the vortex had it too, whipcords of
energy rising from the pit. Kaspar cried
out as he fell, throwing up a desperate
hand...

And someone caught it.

Fingers tightened around his wrist,
pulling him in. With his free hand he
grabbed for the glass floor, clinging on
tight as he dangled over the maelstrom.
Looking up he saw Scratch bending
over him, eyes wide with fear and
excitement as he pulled Kaspar up.

Kaspar scrambled onto the edge of

the platform. Daring a glance back, he saw Darkwing still trying to rise, wings beating desperately against the pull of the vortex. Ashnakh wailed in horror as the raven was dragged down. Kaspar heard a last strangled squawk, then the bird was gone.

The vortex erupted.

A wave of terrible energy burst from it, exploding into the trophy room. Kaspar clung to Scratch's hand as everything howled around them, the whirlpool spinning wildly off its axis, throwing out bolts of magical force. Glass began to shatter, floating panes slamming into one another and exploding in showers of shimmering fragments. The floor tipped and Kaspar felt himself sliding, clinging to Scratch as they skittered and tumbled back towards that yawning gulf. Then just as they were reaching the edge it tipped back the other way, and he was able to struggle to his feet, pulling Scratch with him. Mirrored surfaces burst around them, shards falling in a deadly rain.

Ashnakh floated through the chaos, glass swirling around her. In her coiled hands was another fire-bolt, and her eyes were fixed on Kaspar. 'I suppose I should be proud,' she spat. 'My pupil learns quickly.'

'I had a good teacher,' Kaspar said. 'You showed me things I won't forget as long as I live.'

'And how long will that be?' Ashnakh sneered. 'Ritual be damned. I'm going to kill you, apprentice.'

The ball of energy was growing as she floated towards him, spirits loosed from the maelstrom lashing into her cupped hands. She looked at Kaspar and in the depths of her black eyes he could see nothing but fury and betrayal. He knew that look would haunt his nightmares.

'I'm sorry it had to end this way,' Ashnakh said. 'Of all my victories, this is the bitterest.'

'You haven't won yet,' Kaspar told her,

and glanced up.

A pane of unbroken shadeglass tumbled overhead, and beneath the mirrored surface Kaspar could see figures trapped inside, cloudy eyes staring down as Ashnakh struggled to contain her deadly bolt. The ghost children hammered on the glass, and tiny cracks started to spread.

Then Gethris punched through and the pane disintegrated. The children howled joyfully as they were set free, their shadow-forms spiralling in the air.

They descended on Ashnakh in a boiling mass, screaming as they came. She tried to defend herself but they were already swarming around her, snatching at her clothes, tugging at her like the wind. Her concentration shattered and the fire-bolt exploded in her hands, tearing itself apart in streaks of violet and gold, blistering Ashnakh's skin as she screamed and swiped.

The ghost children peeled away, and

Kaspar heard laughter as they weaved
between the falling mirrors, vanishing
into the pale, cloudless dawn.

Ashnakh fell to her knees, her face
and hands scorched red. She tried to
pick herself up, tried to fashion another
bolt, but her strength was gone. The
glass beneath her began to crack,
jagged splinters running out across
the platform. Then it broke and she
fell, tumbling into the tattered vortex.
Shadows wreathed her falling body,
wrapping around her like a protective

shroud, then she was lost from view.

Kaspar held tight to Scratch, watching as the cracks raced towards them. They backed away, shielding themselves as shards of glass swept through the howling air.

'Come on,' Kaspar said, pulling the boy with him. 'We have to get to the–'

He turned, scanning the trophy room. But the *Arbour Seed* was gone.

CHAPTER TEN

Disintegration

The floor tipped and Kaspar staggered, clinging to Scratch. He could imagine only two possibilities, neither of them good. Either the *Arbour Seed* had failed to fly and had been sucked down into the vortex... or his friends had taken off without him.

The glass platform was rocking and shifting, spinning on its axis as the vortex collapsed. It couldn't be long before it broke and they plummeted down into that unearthly whirlpool.

'Well, we got this far.' Kaspar looked down at Scratch. The boy's face was smeared with dirt and sweat and tiny glass-cut pricks of blood. 'I never thought we would.'

Scratch grinned fiercely, clinging to Kaspar. Then he threw back his head and gave a howl, an animal wail of joy and despair that cut through all the crashing and smashing around them. Kaspar laughed and joined him, and together they howled their lungs out, knowing it would be the last sound they would ever make.

They were creating such a din that Kaspar didn't hear the floor cracking under them, didn't hear the glass circle finally splintering to pieces and dropping into the abyss. He didn't even hear the *Arbour Seed* as it swept in, dodging the panes of glass that still swept through the air. He didn't hear Kiri yelling at him to grab on, and the first he knew was when her hands took hold of him, making him jump.

He looked up in astonishment, clutching Scratch. They were lifted into the air as the floor fell away, the vortex

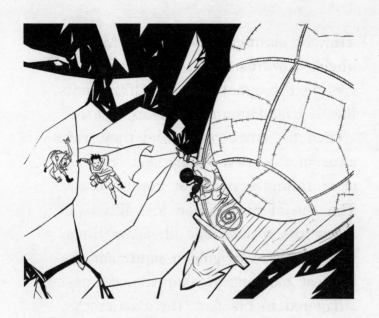

shrieking as the castle broke apart.
Kiri and Thanis hauled Kaspar up by
the collar, with Scratch clinging to his
leg. They both fell into the belly of the
airship, Scratch still howling until Elio
shook him and told him to stop.

Alish stood with both hands on the
wheel, steering between the falling
panes. It was like trying to dodge
between raindrops but somehow she
was managing it, weaving between
a mirror the size of a wall and two
falling, dagger-like shards. Shafts of

sunlight slanted through and Alish angled towards them, the airship's prow cutting through the rain of fragments like a boat through a choppy sea.

Then the wave broke and they were clear of the castle, leaving a trail of spiralling crystals in their wake. The sun of Shyish had just lifted above the rocky ridge ahead of them, bathing them in golden light. For the briefest moment, Kaspar thought as he staggered to his feet, the Battlerock was almost beautiful.

Then something swept past them, a cloud of glittering shadows that tumbled and twisted, heading straight for the ridge and the Realmgate. As it passed, Kaspar thought he heard Gethris's thin, trailing voice crying a thank you.

'Where are they going?' Thanis asked, staring after the spectral children.

'They're going home,' Vertigan told her, dabbing an eye with the sleeve of his robe. 'Just like us.'

The aether-endrin rumbled and Alish

fed in more fuel, checking the dials and
pressure gauges. 'Thanks for coming
back,' Kaspar told her. 'That was some
pretty brave flying.'

Alish blushed. 'Thanks for, you know,
rescuing us from the worst place ever.'

He grinned. 'You're welcome.'

There was a mighty crash and he
looked back to see the Castle of Mirrors
toppling in on itself, panes plummeting,
clouds of glass-dust exploding outwards.
He heard shrieks and bellows amidst
all the noise and thunder, the cry of

countless souls suddenly released from torment. Perhaps in time they would all find their way home.

'We saw Ashnakh fall,' Kiri said. 'She can't have survived that, surely?'

'She's already dead,' Vertigan said, leaning on the airship's railing. 'And she's powerful. No, I don't think we've seen the last of—'

'Look!' Elio interrupted, pointing down. 'There!'

From the clouds of debris a single figure came bounding, a streak of silver weaving over the black rocks. Even from this distance Kaspar could see the red smears on General Bloodspeed's armour, the dents in his breastplate and the fury on his face. But still the soulblight vampire kept moving, darting like mercury through the tumbling labyrinth.

'He's Ashnakh's messenger,' Kaspar told the others. 'He's going to carry word to her forces outside Lifestone, tell them to start the attack. And he's going to bring plenty of reinforcements with him.' He pointed to the army of the dead, standing silently on the slopes. Nighthaunts wailed as they passed over, and soulblight generals called to one another, gesturing into the sky. The skeletal soldiers raised their heads, empty sockets turning to watch as the airship drifted by.

'We need to get to Lifestone before them,' Vertigan said. 'We'll only get one chance to carry out the ritual.'

A purple gleam began to grow on the peak of the ridge and Kaspar saw the tunnel standing wide, waves of sickly iridescence pulsating from it. Alish tweaked a series of gauges and the airship started to descend, making for the opening.

'This ritual,' Kiri said, facing Vertigan. 'What does it do? Isn't it time you told us?'

He sighed, placing a hand on her shoulder. 'It's long past time,' he admitted. 'I should've told you that night at the Arbour, before the Skaven came. Perhaps I should've told each of you when we first met. But it can't be helped now.'

He lifted his head, staring into the beating heart of the Realmgate as they flew closer.

'You see, it all began a very, very long time ago...'

REALMS ARCANA

PART FIVE

THE MORTAL REALMS

Each of the Mortal Realms is a world unto itself, steeped in powerful magic. Seemingly infinite in size, they contain limitless possibilities for discovery and adventure: floating cities and enchanted woodlands, noble beings and dread beasts beyond imagination. But in every corner of every realm, a war rages between the armies of Order and the forces of Chaos. This centuries-long conflict must be won if the realms are to live in peace and freedom.

AZYR

The Realm of Heavens, where the immortal King Sigmar reigns unchallenged.

AQSHY

The Realm of Fire, a region of mighty volcanoes, molten seas and flaming-hot tempers.

GHYRAN

The Realm of Life, where flourishing forests teem with creatures beyond counting.

CHAMON

The Realm of Metal, where rivers of mercury flow through canyons of steel.

SHYISH

The Realm of Death,
a lifeless land where
spirits drift through
silent, shaded tombs.

GHUR

The Realm of
Beasts, where living
monstrosities battle
for dominance.

HYSH

The Realm of Light,
where knowledge
and wisdom are
prized above all.

ULGU

The Realm of
Shadows, a domain
of darkness where
dread phantoms lurk.

SHYISH

Named the Realm of Death, Shyish is
a place of gloom and shadow, haunted
by ghosts and spectres beyond number.
It is not an entirely lifeless land – vast
forests grow here, dark and trackless,
and parts of the realm are inhabited
by communities of mortals: sullen,
unfriendly types scratching a meagre
existence from the soil. There are
even cities in Shyish, like the mighty
Glymmsforge, where forces loyal to the
immortal King Sigmar have forged an
uneasy alliance with the spirits of the
undead.

NAGASH

Known as the Lord of Death, the ancient necromancer Nagash rules over the lands of Shyish. Although he once fought alongside the immortal King Sigmar in the great war between the forces of Order and Chaos, Nagash has now turned wholly to evil. Appearing in many forms, Nagash has power over all the undead beings that haunt the lands of Shyish, including the mighty sorceress Ashnakh, whom he raised from the grave and trained in the necromantic arts.

THE BATTLEROCK

Far out in the Sea of Fading Hope, one of the vast oceans of Shyish, lies the remote island known as the Battlerock. The rock was once the site of a centuries-long conflict, as two great armies fought for control over its most precious resource – a

Realmgate. Beneath the island lies a giant fragment of the mystical crystal warpstone, a shard so large that it has torn a hole in the fabric of reality itself, forming a passage that links Shyish, the Realm of Death, to Ghyran, the Realm of Life. The battle was so fierce that everything living on the island was destroyed, down to the last blade of grass. It's been a barren, lifeless place ever since.

KASPAR

Like his companions, Kaspar bears a birthmark on his wrist that links him to one of the Mortal Realms. In his case the mark is that of Shyish, the Realm of Death – a fact that has both troubled and intrigued Kaspar ever since he learned what the black rune meant. Born in Lifestone and raised on its streets, Kaspar has only hazy memories of his life before he met Thanis and joined the gang of young thieves known as the Scraps. He's a quiet boy, fiercely intelligent but highly secretive – even his closest friends never really know what he's thinking.

ASHNAKH

The powerful undead sorceress Ashnakh has pursued Kaspar and his friends across the Mortal Realms, intending to use them in a mysterious ritual that is somehow connected to their birthmarks. Like Kaspar, Ashnakh also bears the mark of Shyish, the Realm of Death, proving that she, like him, was once a child of Lifestone and the Realm of Ghyran. But Ashnakh has become corrupted by the forces of darkness, and is now utterly in the thrall of the dark lord Nagash.

NIGHTHAUNTS

Nighthaunts are cruel, unquiet spirits raised from the grave by the power of Nagash or one of his underlings. They appear as hooded figures with grasping skeletal fingers, drifting like an unstoppable mist towards their victims. Among the

most feared of the nighthaunts are the chainghasts, wandering spectres bound in links of clanking metal to signify that in life they were prisoners – criminals and reprobates locked up for their ghastly deeds. Other nighthaunts include the Knight of Shrouds, whose terrifying disembodied voice spreads the word of Nagash to his enemies, and the Guardian of Souls, whose dark presence is at the core of any nighthaunt army.

SOULBLIGHT VAMPIRES

Soulblight vampires are among the most powerful and deadly creatures in the Mortal Realms. Immortal beings who feed on blood, they are both physically strong and relentlessly determined, always ready to fight for what they believe is rightfully theirs. Many of Shyish's most powerful kings and queens are soulblights, ruling with an iron fist until they are deposed by a vampire even more cruel and ruthless.

The sorceress Ashnakh employs soulblight generals in her army of the dead, and chief among them is Bloodspeed, an aged and powerful vampire possessed of supernatural swiftness.

THE CASTLE OF MIRRORS

In gratitude for the many victories she won in his name, Nagash granted the sorceress Ashnakh guardianship over the Battlerock and its strategically important Realmgate. Upon this remote island she has raised the Castle of Mirrors, a fortress fashioned from reflective panes of shadeglass, a mystical substance able to capture and imprison the spirits of the dead. In its centre lies the Vortex of Sundered Spirits, a whirlpool of mystical energy powered by the spirits of all those who died on the Battlerock during its epic conflict. Outside the castle Ashnakh has created the Shatterglass Labyrinth, a vast maze of mist and broken mirrors populated by packs of terrifying nighthaunts. Shrouded in an ever-present layer of murky fog, the labyrinth has spells placed upon it to baffle the mind, blur the senses and drive Ashnakh's prisoners mad with fear.

SKELETAL STEEDS

To travel around the Battlerock, the
sorceress Ashnakh summons forth
skeletal steeds, mighty horses built
of bones and held together by dark
magics. Once these proud beasts would
have been warhorses, utilised by the
armies who fought to control the
island. Now they are
merely
fleshless
carcasses,
slaves to
the will of their
terrible mistress.

ABOUT THE AUTHOR

Tom Huddleston is the author of the *Warhammer Adventures: Realm Quest* series, and has also written three instalments in the *Star Wars: Adventures in Wild Space* saga. His other works include the futuristic fantasy adventure story *FloodWorld* and its sequel, *DustRoad*. He lives in East London, and you can find him online at www.tomhuddleston.co.uk.

ABOUT THE ARTISTS

Dan Boultwood is a comic book artist and illustrator from London. When he's not drawing, he collects old shellac records and dances around badly to them in between taking forever to paint his miniatures.

Cole Marchetti is an illustrator and concept artist from California. When he isn't sitting in front of the computer, he enjoys hiking and plein air painting. Warhammer Adventures is his first project working with Games Workshop.

An Extract from book six
Battle for the Soulspring
by Tom Huddleston
(out Summer 2021)

'It was the Sylvaneth who healed
me,' Vertigan explained, leaning over
the side of the airship and gazing
into the tangled forest below. Strange
cries echoed from the twisted trees
and shimmering light danced in the
depths. 'Without Litheroot I would've
been lost. Not dead, perhaps, like the
others. But gone, nonetheless.'

Kiri heard deep sadness in the old
man's voice, and his face was drawn
and weary. But at least now she

understood her purpose, the reason she and her friends had been drawn together. They had to return to the Arbour, open the Soulspring and save the city of Lifestone before it was overrun by the sorceress Ashnakh and her army of the dead.

Alish stood at the wheel, steadying the *Arbour Seed* as night winds buffeted the little airship. The others perched on the benches to either side, silently pondering everything Vertigan had told them. Scratch shivered, huddling close to Kaspar, while Thanis sat upright in the prow, gazing out into the night. Barely any time had passed since they'd toppled Ashnakh's tower and escaped from the Realm of Death. Already, Kiri knew, the sorceress would be recovering her strength and marshalling her forces.

'Why did Aisha do it?' Elio asked. 'Who gave her the power?'

'It was Nagash,' Vertigan spat. 'The

great necromancer, Aisha's true master. Like you, she was born in Lifestone, the child of ordinary market traders. But her parents were taken when she was very young, I could never discover exactly how. She was left in the care of an ageing relative – a petty conjuror, little better than a woods witch. But the old woman was a follower of Nagash, and hoping to impress him she took this chosen child under her wing, giving her the secret name of Ashnakh and raising her in the ways of Death, encouraging her to use the power of her birthmark. Their intention was to corrupt the ritual, to poison the Soulspring and allow Nagash to claim the soul of Lifestone for himself. A great prize indeed.'

'But you stopped her,' Kiri said. 'You broke the spell.'

'I did.' Vertigan nodded. 'I wasn't the only one who'd been training in secret. I'd become fascinated by the arcane arts, and had begun to learn all I could about the life of a witch hunter. I had just enough willpower to resist her, but I was the only one who could. The others lost their lives, Aisha included. It was Nagash who brought her back, returning her spirit so she could complete her task, find the next generation of marked children and corrupt the ritual again. We are the only ones who can stop her.'

'Why didn't you tell us before?' Kiri asked. 'Why the secrecy?'

'Tradition,' Vertigan sighed. 'The truth was always hidden until the morning of the ritual. And I suppose I was afraid, too. Afraid that if you learned the truth too soon, if you realised how much danger you were in, you might be too scared to continue. I should've known better.'

There was a sudden screech in the dark, a blood-chilling cry echoing above the trees. They heard the thrum of wings and Kiri saw a hideous shape in the moonlight, a scaly, lizard-like form soaring on ragged pinions. Its black body was ridged with bony growths and its jaw was spiked with monstrous fangs.

'That's a terrorgheist,' Elio shuddered. 'I saw a picture of one once and it scared the life out of me. I never wanted to see one for real.'

Thanis peered closer. 'There's someone riding on it,' she said in awe. A saddle was strapped to the creature's frame, a silver figure clasping the leather harness.

'General Bloodspeed,' Kaspar said. 'He's Ashnakh's messenger. She sent him to alert her troops and start the attack.'

The soulblight vampire had spotted them – Kiri saw his blue lips draw back over pointed teeth, his bone-white skin shining in the moonlight. Then he snapped the reins and the terrorgheist surged forward, its barbed tail lashing behind it.

'Sigmar's hammer, why didn't he attack us?' Alish asked. 'That thing could've smashed us out of the sky.'

'He's scared,' Thanis sneered. 'Seven against one. He's a coward.'

But Kaspar shook his head. 'Ashnakh ordered him not to hurt us, remember? She wants us in Lifestone. She wants us to carry out the ritual, so she can poison it again. So she and her dark master can steal the soul of the city.'

'So why are we doing it?' Elio asked. 'Why don't we just fly away somewhere she can't find us?'

'Because that would doom Lifestone forever,' Vertigan told him. 'The city must be restored or it will fade utterly, and one of the jewels of Ghyran will fall into ruin.'

'So we need to make sure we're prepared,' Kiri said determinedly. 'When she comes for us, we have to be ready to fight back.'

'Remember what Litheroot told us,'

Thanis put in. 'She said if we could find Aisha's childhood home, we might discover something that could help us. Some way to weaken her. Do you think that's true, Master Vertigan?'

The old man pursed his lips thoughtfully. 'I looked for the place myself, but I could never find it. I came to suspect that Aisha had... well, that she had *warned* the house to watch out for me. Left a charm that hid it from my sight. You might have more luck. But it's still one house in an entire city, where will you start looking?'

Elio sighed nervously. 'I'm supposed to ask my father to give us access to the Archives. But you know, he might not help us. The last time we spoke it didn't go so well. He told me I wasn't his son any more.'

'But you've changed,' Kiri told him. 'Maybe he has too. And anyway, I'll come with you. To help persuade him.'

Elio's eyes narrowed. 'Don't shoot

him with your catapult or anything, will you?'

'I'll come too,' Kaspar said. 'I know Ashnakh best, if we're looking for something that connects to her, I might be able to spot it.'

'So what about the rest of us?' Thanis asked. 'Do you think we should all go?'

Vertigan shook his head. 'Someone must go to the Arbour and prepare for dawn,' he said, scanning the black horizon. 'I only hope we will have enough time.'

Beneath them the trees were beginning to thin out, and off in the distance Kiri could see the line of torches marking the outer walls of Lifestone. But between them and the city was a black gulf, the valley below dark and silent.

'Where's Ashnakh's army?' she whispered. 'Are they gone?'

No one spoke, and for a moment the only sound was the droning of the airship's aether-endrins. Then Thanis pointed, and Kiri saw a moving speck, glittering silver as it soared from shadow into moonlight. The terrorgheist beat its wings, descending into the valley. And as it did so, a terrible cry went up.

The roar echoed from the steep slopes on either side, bellowing and howling and cursing in a hundred hideous tongues. Light bloomed below them, lines of sickly violet radiance erupting from the heart of the valley and spreading like vines. And everywhere it touched Kiri saw movement – corpse-warriors and skeletal steeds, soulblight regiments and shrouded banks of half-formed nighthaunts, all marching into position.

Bloodspeed landed his monstrous steed in the centre of the valley, torches flaring around him. He pointed one gloved hand towards the city and the dead army howled, turning to face the high shield walls of Lifestone. The earth shook as they started to advance, their feet pounding the dust, their siege engines groaning as they rolled over the stony ground.

'There's so many of them,' Thanis said in horror. 'The city'll be overrun long before daybreak.'